"Didn't that extraordinary young man with the beard mention noises last night in the woods? We have a man upstairs with three bullet wounds in him, and he must have been shot nearby. He certainly couldn't have walked far. . . ."

Sister Hyacinthe looked at her accusingly. "Sister John, you're enjoying this!"

"I used to adore crossword puzzles," confessed Sister John. "Let's have a look in the barn, it won't take but a moment."

Sister Hyacinthe sighed. "I've driven several hundred miles today, Sister John, I've pulled money out of a well and a bleeding man out of a closet and we've still not had our supper."

Sister John absently patted her arm. "Just a glance," she promised, and strode across the lawn, skirts flying.

By Dorothy Gilman
Published by Fawcett Books:

UNCERTAIN VOYAGE
A NUN IN THE CLOSET
THE CLAIRVOYANT COUNTESS
THE TIGHTROPE WALKER
INCIDENT AT BADAMYÂ
CARAVAN
THE BELLS OF FREEDOM
THE MAZE IN THE HEART OF THE CASTLE
GIRL IN BUCKSKIN

The Mrs. Pollifax series
THE UNEXPECTED MRS. POLLIFAX
THE AMAZING MRS. POLLIFAX
THE ELUSIVE MRS. POLLIFAX
A PALM FOR MRS. POLLIFAX
MRS. POLLIFAX ON SAFARI
MRS. POLLIFAX ON THE CHINA STATION
MRS. POLLIFAX AND THE HONG KONG BUDDHA
MRS. POLLIFAX AND THE GOLDEN TRIANGLE
MRS. POLLIFAX AND THE WHIRLING DERVISH
MRS. POLLIFAX AND THE SECOND THIEF
MRS. POLLIFAX PURSUED
MRS. POLLIFAX AND THE LION KILLER
MRS. POLLIFAX, INNOCENT TOURIST

Nonfiction
A NEW KIND OF COUNTRY

A NUN IN THE CLOSET

Dorothy Gilman

FAWCETT CREST • NEW YORK

A Fawcett Crest Book
Published by Ballantine Books
Copyright © 1975 by Dorothy Gilman Butters

ISBN 0-449-21167-3

Selection of the Literary Guild/Young Adult Division, January 1975
Selection of the Catholic Digest Book Club
Selection of the Walter J. Black Detective Book Club

This edition published by arrangement with Doubleday & Company, Inc.

Manufactured in the United States of America

First Fawcett Crest Edition: March 1976
First Ballantine Books Edition: February 1983

OPM 45 44 43 42 41 40 39 38 37 36

For
LARRY ASHMEAD
and
BETTY BARTELME

Prologue

At the Abbey of St. Tabitha the sisters met to discuss gravely which of the seventeen among them should leave the abbey and go out into the world to look over the property so astonishingly bequeathed to them. Upper New York State lay only a few hundred miles from the abbey but the sisters were aware that the trip could be perilous—word had filtered through to them of Inflation and Muggings—and it was difficult to think which of them was seasoned enough to go. They were not without worldly accomplishments: Sister Vincent played the lute, and had composed several original pieces; Sister Beatrice illuminated manuscripts that blossomed like flowers under her brush; Sister Maria wrote exquisite poems for the small magazine they printed three times a year but none of these gifts was felt to be exactly right for the assessing of "one hundred and fifty acres with house in disrepair" that the mysterious Mr. Moretti had left to them.

Theirs was a democratic order, and after prayer and reflection the sisters each wrote a name on a slip of paper and handed it to the abbess. She read them aloud, one by one. "Sister John ... Sister John ... Sister John ..." When she had finished there were seventeen votes for Sister John, which did not surprise her; she had often thought that if souls could be captured and pinned like butterflies Sister John's soul would have a width and a breadth to outdo them all. It would also, she thought dryly, have particularly exuberant colors.

"Well then," said the recipient of seventeen votes, "I shall choose Sister Hyacinthe to go with me, if I may."

There was a start of astonishment among them at this, and fourteen pairs of eyes moved to Sister Hyacinthe, who sat in the corner, and then fourteen pairs of eyes fled guiltily elsewhere.

"A very sensible decision," announced the abbess.

Because, she wrote that night to their mother-house in Switzerland, *when we run out of money Sister Hyacinthe knows how to make a very good dinner out of herbs, weeds, and ground nuts. Sister John, of course, is the only one who can mend our printing press when it breaks down.*

These skills, she thought, were surely potent enough to confront the world for which they prayed each morning at Matins, before they weeded the vegetable garden and while the bread was baking.

St. Tabitha's had been a part of the rolling green Pennsylvania countryside since 1955, when it had been invited to the United States by a bishop whom nobody could remember now but who had probably been impressed by the fact that the small Swiss order lived by the simple rules of St. Benedict, insisted upon autonomy and would never appeal for any funds. It was Mother Clothilde who crossed the Atlantic to establish the order, and within two years the abbey had gained eighteen American sisters; this, however, proved to be its peak year. In those early days a primitive septic tank was a recurring problem, and Mother Clothilde made the mistake of digging it out personally, with the help of Sister Emma. Both sisters succumbed to serum hepatitis within the week. No new sisters came to join them, and the remaining seventeen survived the passing years by sewing altar cloths, printing their small devotional magazine called *Reflections*, growing their own vegetables and baking and selling bread.

It was the bread that saved them. Quite suddenly in 1968 it became a gourmet item in the nearest community—due entirely to something called health foods, which the sisters found incomprehensible—and now each morning, promptly at half-past six, one of Mr. Armisbruck's vans arrived to carry away sixty loaves of freshly baked bread, thirty of which went to his delicatessen in northern Bridgemont, and thirty to his shop in Bridgemont Corners. It was on the heels of this modest solvency that news came of the property bequeathed to them by a total stranger named Joseph Moretti.

"Did he really like our bread so much?" asked Sister Hyacinthe, in whose mind one miracle was connected with another.

"We have no idea," confessed the abbess. "The lawyer, Mr. Cherpin, is kindness itself about describing the property and sending maps, but he flatly ignores all my questions about Mr. Moretti. Since so few people know of our existence it's all very puzzling."

Sister John said promptly, "How do we get to New York State without any money?" She had a practical mind that went at once to the point.

It was to Mr. Armisbruck, a Lutheran, that they took this problem, and Mr. Armisbruck listened attentively over a cup of alfalfa tea while the abbess explained the facts of the legacy. There were not only the one hundred and fifty acres, she pointed out, but there was the house, too, which was thought to be furnished. An inventory would be necessary. . . .

Land was something that Mr. Armisbruck understood at once. "How much money have you for the trip?"

The abbess turned to Sister Maria, who said without hesitation, "Nineteen dollars and sixty-three cents."

Mr. Armisbruck considered the situation, aware of seventeen pairs of eyes watching him. The solution, he said at last, was quite simple. If one of the sisters would learn how to drive, and if they would consider increasing the number of loaves they baked to seventy, he would be glad to lend them one of his bright red Armisbruck Delicatessen delivery vans. If they would also put in a word for his family in their daily prayers —Mr. Armisbruck was a man who liked to cover all his bets—he would throw in a full tank of gas and make a contribution of twenty-five dollars to the order.

The sisters were delighted by such a rain of miracles after years of drought. Driving lessons were subsequently given Sister Hyacinthe by the delivery boy. Mr. Armisbruck's van was packed with five loaves of bread (Baked Fresh Every Day at the Abbey of St. Tabitha); with two bedrolls, a shovel, a flashlight, a box of Sister Hyacinthe's healing herbs, a soup kettle, a few books and the deed to the Moretti property.

On the sixth day of July the sisters lined up along the driveway under the maple trees to wave good-by to Sisters John and Hyacinthe. The van pulled away, narrowly missing a sycamore and tumbling a post in the fence as it turned into the main road.

"*Benedicamus domino*," said the abbess.

"*Deo gratias*," responded the sisters.

1

Sister Hyacinthe was as dark as Sister John was fair, given to small superstitions, a certain amount of brooding that drew her brows together frequently, and a tendency to expect the worst. There was Indian blood in her background and this gave her cheekbones prominence and her skin a dark cast. She had been raised in impoverished hill country, her only contact with culture a group of Catholic nuns working among the poor. There was, or so Mother Clothilde had said, not a great deal to *do* with her.

Except enjoy her, Sister John had pointed out, but she appeared to be the only one who appreciated Sister Hyacinthe's fey qualities.

Sister John had never found anyone threatening; it was not in her nature, which was cheerful and abundantly optimistic. Nothing was impossible, she felt, if one only had faith. Sister Vincent said that she was like a silver bell, .999 pure, that always struck the right note. If at times this was tiresome to live with it was leavened by her competence, which was formidable, and her eagerness, which could be misplaced but was always ardent. Physically she was as luminous to look at as a Renoir.

Sister Hyacinthe, on the other hand, was pure Gauguin, and when the sisters of St. Tabitha prayed for the capacity to love God's less fortunate creatures it was frequently she who came unbidden to their minds. In the early days Mother Clothilde had tried her on sewing but her stitches were wild and she absentmindedly sewed altar cloths to her lap. She was indifferent to reading and to writing; she was a hazard in the kitchen and when Sister Vincent played Bach she fell asleep. Only with growing things did she feel at home, and it was the present abbess, more pragmatic than Clothilde, who reasoned that if this was her only gift then she might as well become an accomplished botanist, learning the scientific names of plants as well as their uses.

During the trip into New York State it became obvious that driving was not going to be added to Sister Hyacinthe's small list of skills. Sister John decided that Mr. Armisbruck's delivery boy must have been an incipient speed demon and the licensing examiner distraught when he tested her, for there was a distinctly erratic quality to her driving. They were stopped three times by policemen, once for driving only twenty miles an hour on the thruway, a second time for driving over eighty miles an hour, while a third police car overtook them with sirens shrieking because Sister Hyacinthe had seen skullcap and puffballs growing beside the thruway and parked to gather a few plants.

"There seem to be a great many regulations," said Sister John when this crisis had been met. "What was it he thought you were collecting?"

"Cannabis sativa," Sister Hyacinthe told her indig-

nantly. "I explained that it was *Scutellaria lateriflora*
but he said you couldn't trust anybody these days."

"Strange," said Sister John, and returned to her map,
which suggested that presently they would leave the
thruway behind them. It was a thought that pleased her
because she knew God watched over them but she
couldn't help feeling that Sister Hyacinthe's driving
must tax Him to the limit.

By four o'clock, however, they had mercifully exchanged the thruway for Route 9-W. By half-past the
hour they were in Gatesville asking directions to Fallen
Stump Road, and five miles later Sister Hyacinthe drew
up under a sign that read FALLEN STUMP ROAD. "I'm tired
and my plants need water," she announced. "Are we
nearly there?"

They peered down a country road that looked abandoned by all but postmen, lovers and Boy Scouts. The
limbs of trees, heavy with dust and heat, hung low over
an oiled dirt surface, and from the bushes came the
keening of locusts. "According to the lawyer's map,"
said Sister John, "the Moretti property is bounded on
three sides by this road."

Sister Hyacinthe looked expectantly into the wall of
laurel on the right.

"According to his written directions," went on Sister
John, "there's a road into the property nine tenths of a
mile further along."

"Like a treasure hunt," said Sister Hyacinthe, nodding, and drove the van on down the road until her
companion, eyes on the odometer, cried, "Stop!"

"Over there," said Sister John, pointing to a gap in
the laurel and there, in just the right place, stood a pair
of stone pillars almost totally obscured by ivy. Sister

John climbed down and crossed the road and a moment later plucked a fallen mailbox from the grass. Time and weather had bleached most of the printing on it but the last four letters remained, and they were unquestionably e-t-t-i. "I think we're here," she called to Sister Hyacinthe. "Aim the van between the pillars and let's see what's on the other side."

A small jungle of undergrowth and a graveled driveway lay on the other side, and then the laurel thinned and they came out on a huge expanse of lawn grown wild with yellow mustard. At the crest of the lawn, some distance to their right, stood a house that bristled with turrets, gingerbread, eaves, gables and porches.

"But it's beautiful!" gasped Sister John. "Look at its size, Sister Hyacinthe, the view, the trees—this isn't a property, it's an estate."

Sister Hyacinthe's glance was skeptical. "Mmmm," she murmured noncommittally, and shifted gears, steered the van around a curve past a secondary drive that led to a barn and drew up beside the sagging front porch. The porch ran the width of the house, laced with thick wisteria vines knotted like macrame and beaded here and there with fading purple blossoms. As the engine died there was silence except for a low murmur from the thruway, which they could see winding like a serpent across the valley on their left.

"How wonderfully peaceful," murmured Sister John.

Sister Hyacinthe turned and gave her a curious glance. "Something moved in one of the upstairs windows, you know."

"Nonsense, Sister Hyacinthe, the house has been unoccupied for years."

"Something moved," she said stubbornly. "I saw it when we stopped back there to look."

"A curtain perhaps. There may be a window cracked or broken so that the wind blows through the house."

"There isn't any wind."

Sister John's glance was patient; it was she, after all, who insisted that Sister Hyacinthe kept them from being like peas in a pod (or like *Pisum Leguminosae*, she would add wryly). "A trick of light, then. The sun on the window."

"Or Mr. Moretti," said Sister Hyacinthe, crossing herself. "Doesn't it strike you as odd how little that lawyer would tell us about him?"

"Yes, but the lawyer made it plain that he's *dead*."

"Even worse," Sister Hyacinthe said, nodding. "The house is haunted, I feel it. Just see how dark it is and how the trees scrape against the windows. I *know* something moved upstairs, we'll go inside and Mr. Moretti will be walking the halls and what do we do then?"

"Thank him for bequeathing the house to St. Tabitha's," said Sister John briskly, "and then say in a polite but firm voice 'in the name of Jesus Christ go away,' which I believe is what one says to ghosts. Now are you going to come inside with me, Sister Hyacinthe, or sit here crossing yourself all afternoon?"

"I'll come," Sister Hyacinthe said gloomily.

Sister John picked up the long skirts of her blue cotton habit and ran lightly up the steps, opened a creaking screen door and inserted a key into the massive door behind it. Sister Hyacinthe followed nervously. The door gave a groan of protest, shuddered, opened and Sister John led the way into the hall.

Inside they stopped, taken aback by the opaque flat

silence of the house. On either side of the hall loomed a dark and cavernous room; instinctively they turned toward the living room, whose far wall contained the more windows. The windows only faintly relieved the darkness, however, for ivy and wisteria had woven intricate patterns across the glass, blotting out all daylight except tiny cnips of brilliance no larger than coins. In this green twilight Sister John and Sister Hyacinthe exchanged glances.

"Grim," admitted Sister John.

"But look, there's light somewhere," cried Sister Hyacinthe, and plunged joyfully across the main hall and down a passageway to follow dimness a shade lighter than the murk of the hall. Passing a succession of doors she emerged into blinding sunshine that came from a single window in a room at the back of the house. It was a kitchen, lined with ancient wooden cupboards and a tin sink. "Thank God—sunlight," she said fervently.

Sister John, following, stepped to a light switch, flicked it and when overhead illumination blended with the sunlight said with relief, "And *I* thank God for electricity, considering the fact that it'll be dark in a few hours ... Sister Hyacinthe, we'd better unpack while it's still daylight. We'll have bread for supper, some of Sister Scholastica's cheese and one of your herb teas."

"Valerian, I think," said Sister Hyacinthe. "It soothes the nerves."

They carried in bedrolls, the flashlight, food and the box of herbs, turning on lights as they went, lights that showed the living room to be not empty at all but crammed with shapes that looked like a herd of sheeted animals encamped for the night. Sister John unwrapped

their supplies and began to slice bread at one corner of
the kitchen table while Sister Hyacinthe hunted for a
pail to fill with water for her plants. After opening the
door of a broom closet, and then a pantry, she opened
a third door and disappeared. From somewhere in the
back she called, "There was a garden out here once. I
can transplant my herbs tomorrow."

Her voice grew louder and she reappeared carrying a
bucket. Moving to the sink she turned the faucet,
twisted it back and forth, and said in exasperation, "Sister John, there's no water."

Sister John looked up. "Nonsense, there's electricity."

"Yes, but no water."

Together they attacked the spigot, which turned easily
enough but produced only squeaks and a hollow rattling
of pipes. "There has to be water somewhere," protested
Sister Hyacinthe.

"The turn-on is probably in the cellar," Sister John
said with a notable lack of enthusiasm.

"I don't think I could bear the cellar yet," confessed
Sister Hyacinthe. "I saw a well in the garden, an old
stone well with a roof over it, but there might be water
in it, enough at least for my herbs. If there's more we
can boil it for drinking." She looked at Sister John defiantly. "My plants simply have to be watered or they'll
die from the heat."

"Then of course you must water them," agreed Sister
John.

They carried the box of herbs and the bucket down
wooden steps to a bricked path that encircled what must
have been a kitchen garden. In the center of the circle
stood the well, surrounded by beds of weeds and earth,
a birdbath and a rusted iron bench. A private hedge en-

closed this domesticated circle, but the hedge, like everything else, had given up the ghost long since and grown wild.

"Throw a pebble," suggested Sister Hyacinthe.

Sister Hyacinthe tossed a handful of gravel down the well and listened. "It splashed," she said, and bending over the wall peered inside. "Something's already down there, Sister John, but it doesn't look like a bucket." Turning, she looked at Sister John and then beyond her and gave a startled cry.

A bearded young man stood just inside the privet hedge watching them. He wore an Indian headband across his forehead, a pair of faded blue jeans, nothing more, and his hair and beard were a bright ginger red. "Did I frighten you?" he asked.

"No," gasped Sister Hyacinthe.

"Yes," said Sister John calmly. "We didn't hear you."

"I came by the path through the woods," he said, gesturing vaguely behind the privet hedge. "Would you believe I didn't even know there was a house here?"

"I could believe it," said Sister Hyacinthe, nodding.

He looked puzzled. "You're not camping out, too, are you? I mean—*nuns?*"

"In a manner of speaking we're camping out, yes. Nuns do, you know. They *can.*"

"I'm Unitarian myself," he said. "We're camped about half a mile away on Fallen Stump Road—four of us, usually, except when Bhanjan Singh comes. We heard these noises last night in the woods, I promised the girls I'd check them out."

"Noises?" said Sister John.

He nodded. "Some kid fooling around with Fourth of

July firecrackers could start a hell of a fire in the woods. Naomi?"

A girl magically appeared behind him, slim as a reed, copper-colored hair reaching to her waist and a shapeless muslin dress curling around her ankles. "Hey," she said, "nuns," and two against two they measured each other across the tangle of weeds until the girl's glance dropped to the box of plants at Sister Hyacinthe's feet.

"Herbs?" she cried and politeness vanished. Naomi flew across the path and dropped to the ground, crossing her legs under her and displaying a pair of remarkably dirty feet. "That's sage," she said, poking it with a long finger. "Hey, you've got rosemary and skullcap and—is this comfrey?"

"Yes," said Sister Hyacinthe, and smiled. The effect was startling. Some people smile easily: Sister John gave the impression of smiling all the time because the corners of her mouth turned up, and even when she was not smiling there was a radiance about her. Sister Hyacinthe's face, on the other hand, was all angles, dark and stubbornly secretive. When she smiled it was an event that very nearly took the breath away.

Naomi, regarding the transformation with astonishment, said, "You must be really into them."

"Into them?"

"Care about herbs."

"Sister Hyacinthe is very gifted with them," said Sister John. "She cured Sister Thecla of asthma and Sister Charity of arthritis, and her sorrel omelet is an aesthetic experience. She dries them, too."

"Dries them!" The girl stared at Sister Hyacinthe in awe. "Would you show us how? Could you give us tips?"

"Tips?" repeated Sister Hyacinthe.

"Like in horse racing," said Sister John, and held out her hand. "If we're neighbors I think we should introduce ourselves. I'm Sister John and this is Sister Hyacinthe from St. Tabitha's Abbey in Bridgemont, Pennsylvania. Mr. Moretti left this house and one hundred and fifty acres to St. Tabitha's and we've come to look it over."

The young man's gaze lifted to the house, his eyes following the scallops of gingerbread around the eaves and up the turrets. "A real spook house, isn't it? Just the two of you?"

"Just the two of us."

He thrust out his hand. "I'm Brill Stevenson. Naomi—?"

"Naomi Witkowski," she said, standing up and brushing grass from her skirt. "We have chickens, you know, we can sell you some eggs. Have you been camping here long?"

Sister John glanced at her watch. "Sixty-five minutes."

Brill grinned. "Oh—well then. No use asking if firecrackers woke you up last night, we'll be on our way again. Look, it's great meeting you but we've got to go and look around some more. Maybe you'd like to stop in and see us soon. Considering," he added dryly, "it's probably your land we're camped on."

"Oh, I do hope we'll meet again," Sister Hyacinthe said in a rare burst of enthusiasm. "Come for a cup of goldenrod tea."

"Goldenrod tea," breathed Naomi. "Oh, beautiful. We're trying to live off the land, you know. I can't say we're very successful yet but—"

"Naomi."

"Oh—coming, brute," she said, and blowing them a kiss she followed her companion through the privet hedge and vanished.

Sister Hyacinthe said in an awed voice, "He looked just like John the Baptist."

"And the girl like a gypsy. Perhaps some kind of tribal custom," Sister John said, puzzled. "Boy Scouts never used to look like that. Are you ready to draw the water now?"

"I liked them," Sister Hyacinthe said, turning reluctantly back to the well, and they grasped the iron handle, which resisted them until Sister John leaned on it, and then the chain clanked away noisily, bringing up what felt like a large container. As it neared the top, Sister Hyacinthe's eyes widened. "What on earth can it be?" she protested. Two more turns of the crank and a completely dry old suitcase arrived at the surface. Sister John reached out and swung it over the top while Sister Hyacinthe disengaged the chain. "What a ridiculous thing to put down a well!"

"And completely dry," said Sister John, puzzled. She leaned forward to stare up into the peaked roof. "Ingenious," she said, pointing. "Look, there's a pulley wheel here with metal teeth, and a stick was inserted to keep the suitcase above water level." She reached up and drew out a broken stick. "That's why we had trouble turning the crank at first. I wonder what's inside it. What kind of moss is growing on it?"

"That's not moss, it's lichen," said Sister Hyacinthe, and attaching her empty bucket to the chain she began turning the crank again. "It's padlocked, too, as you can see."

"Yes, but under the lichen it's genuine cowhide. A good scrubbing and a little sunshine and it would make a lovely case for Sister Vincent's lute." Sister John regarded it thoughtfully. "It all depends on whether there's mildew inside. Have you water yet?"

"Almost," gasped Sister Hyacinthe, reeling up the chain.

"Then I just might see . . . the padlock shouldn't be any problem, it's rusty." She carried the suitcase to the bench, placed a knee across it to steady it and hit the padlock with a sharp rock. On the third attempt the padlock snapped and fell to the bricked path. Sister Hyacinthe, bringing up a bucket brimming with water, put it down on the flagstone and came to watch. Sister John opened the suitcase, removed a crumpled New York *Daily News* and exposed its contents.

"Holy Mother of God," gasped Sister Hyacinthe.

"Why, that dear Mr. Moretti," said Sister John warmly, "he's left us money as well as a house. Look, Sister Hyacinthe—a whole suitcase of money."

The bills had been crammed into the suitcase in a very untidy manner, some of them crisp, some of them worn. Sister John reached out and plucked one from the pile. "A twenty-dollar bill," she said in a hushed voice. "Just think how long it's been since we've seen one. Here's a fifty, a hundred, and three more hundreds. They're real, Sister Hyacinthe, just look at them."

"I *am* looking at them," said Hyacinthe, "but are you sure they're meant for us?"

Sister John smiled at her forgivingly. "One should never doubt miracles, Sister Hyacinthe. Mr. Moretti's legacy included all the furnishings, didn't it? And the well," she added reasonably, "simply happens to be furnished with money."

"It seems a very peculiar place to leave it."

"There are men like that, they don't trust banks. Have you thought what this means, Sister Hyacinthe?"

"Trouble," hazarded Sister Hyacinthe.

Her eyes were glowing. "Nonsense, it means a new oven for St. Tabitha's, perhaps even a new roof, and then there's the Missionary Fund—" She sank down beside the suitcase, the voluminous skirts of her habit surrounding her like petals of a blue flower, a rapt look on her face. "We were guided here, Sister Hyacinthe, God works in mysterious ways His wonders to perform."

"Mr. Moretti too," pointed out Sister Hyacinthe. "Look, there's a breeze stirring up, Sister John, the bills will blow all over the garden, and we've had nothing to eat yet—"

Sister John promptly closed the suitcase. "How selfish of me," she sighed. "It just proves how quickly money corrupts, I'm afraid I was even thinking of a new printing press." She picked up the suitcase and waited while Sister Hyacinthe sprinkled water over her herbs and then they stoically struggled toward the house, Sister John with the suitcase, Sister Hyacinthe with her half-filled bucket of water. Stopping in the middle of the kitchen to catch her breath, Sister John said, "I'll write to the abbess about this tonight." She carried the suitcase into the pantry and with only one last wistful glance placed it under a shelf lined with glass jars of sugar. But not happily, for ideas were blossoming in her fertile mind like flowers.

Back in the kitchen she found Sister Hyacinthe pouring water from the bucket into the soup kettle. "The stove works?"

"Mercifully, yes. What's that in your hand?"

"The New York *Daily News* from the suitcase, it's dated December 12, 1963. Sister Hyacinthe, do you suppose that's the day the money was put down the well?" Meeting Sister Hyacinthe's skeptical glance she said, "Well, it could be, I don't see why not. It seems a very logical deduction."

She smoothed out the crumpled news sheet while Sister Hyacinthe sliced the goat's cheese. This and the water beginning to bubble on the stove were the only sounds, and then abruptly Sister Hyacinthe dropped her knife and stared at Sister John with widened eyes. "Holy Mother of God, what was *that*?"

Sister John stood very still, listening. "It was a thump. Something fell."

"But it came from upstairs, Sister John."

"Yes, I know."

"Chairs don't move around by themselves," Sister Hyacinthe told her desperately. "Beds don't move, either. To make a thump something has to move."

"Or someone," said Sister John, and they both stared at the ceiling from which the noise had come.

2

After a short pause Sister Hyacinthe said, "You're getting a funny expression on your face, Sister John. I have the feeling you're going to be terribly brave in a minute and I can't bear it."

"But we have to, you know. We have to go up and see what it is."

"*I* don't have to," said Sister Hyacinthe.

"It's a matter of alternatives," pointed out Sister John. "I'm experiencing the greatest reluctance to sleep in a house that has thumps. Where's your faith, Sister Hyacinthe?"

"Back at St. Tabitha's, where I'd like to be right now."

"Yes, but we're not at St. Tabitha's, we've entered the world," Sister John told her firmly. "We have to expect certain oddities. It isn't as if we have to go upstairs unarmed, you know, there's a heavy iron skillet hanging on the wall behind you, and I can take the carving knife, because I'm sure God appreciates whatever help we give Him. I think, Sister Hyacinthe, that we've got to go upstairs."

Sister Hyacinthe shivered but reluctantly followed
her into the main hall. Lifting her skirts, Sister John led
the way up the wide mahogany stairs to the second
floor, turning on lights as she met them, the carving
knife in her right hand, the flashlight in her left. The
hall upstairs was spacious, running the width of the
house and broad enough to entertain two alcoves with
window seats and several niches for potted plants. Only
two ceiling lights worked, and feebly, but it was nevertheless brighter up here, the wisteria having dissipated
most of its energy in the climb to the porch roof.
Through a wide bow window on the landing they could
see the thruway, its cars like small bugs racing from
north to south and south to north.

"The thump came from over the kitchen," whispered
Sister Hyacinthe, pointing down the hall to the right.

Sister John nodded but calmly turned to the left and
began a methodical search of each room. The hall was
carpeted and their steps muted. She opened the door to
a large bedroom and Sister Hyacinthe opened the door
to a linen closet. They discovered five large bedrooms,
all of them furnished with huge beds and chiffoniers,
and after inspecting each of them they came at last to
the room at the end of the hall over the kitchen. Here
Sister John bowed her head and silently moved her lips.
Sister Hyacinthe urgently crossed herself, held up her
frying pan and pushed open the door.

The room was small and dark; it was also empty of
furniture. There was a solitary window at the rear and
four doors lining one side, but Sister Hyacinthe immediately found it ominous that the light bulb had been removed from the socket on the wall. Sister John turned

on the flashlight, crossed the room to the farthest door and opened it.

"Closet," she said, bumping into Sister Hyacinthe as she turned. "Sister Hyacinthe, don't look so frightened, there's nothing here."

"All right, all right," Sister Hyacinthe said crossly, and took the flashlight and opened the second door. "Turret," she announced, looking at narrow dark wooden stairs curving out of sight. "There must be a tremendous view up there, Sister John." Encouraged, she opened the next door and stood a long time staring inside. After an interval she said, *"Oh,"* and then Sister John heard her say in a strangled voice. "In the name of Jesus Christ go away in the name of Jesus Christ go away in the—"

Sister John walked to her side, glanced into the closet and drew in her breath sharply.

"—name of Jesus Christ go away. In the name of—"

"But he's not a ghost," said Sister John. "At least his foot just moved. I think he's alive." She removed the flashlight from Sister Hyacinthe's trembling hand and directed it at the man slumped against the wall of the closet. "He's unconscious," she said in astonishment.

Sister Hyacinthe stopped her incantations and looked. "Holy Mother of God," she whispered, and slipped to her knees beside the man. "Move the light to his face," she said, and placed a hand on either of his cheeks. "Clammy," she told Sister John. Her fingers flew to his pulse and then to the collar of his shirt to loosen it. When she drew back she held her hand up to the light and stared at the wet red stickiness dripping from her fingers. "Blood?" she faltered.

"Yes," said Sister John, adding unsteadily, "He can't stay in the closet."

"No," agreed Sister Hyacinthe.

"Stay with him," said Sister John, and fled the room to return with a light bulb that she screwed into the empty socket.

Illumination did not bring enlightenment, however; the man looked no less corpse-like in the light of a twenty-watt bulb, and there remained no suitable explanation for his being in the closet of an abandoned house. There was a smear of blood on his forehead and a scarlet line under his ear, but these were minor compared to the alarming amount of blood staining the sleeve of his left arm; he was drenched with it from elbow to shoulder. They patted his pockets for a clue to his identity but found not so much as a wallet or a slip of paper. As for his appearance, it was as nondescript as his clothes and made more so by the stubble of a gray beard. Only his condition was identifiable: it was precarious.

They hastily dragged a mattress down the hall, covered it with a sheet from the linen closet and loosely knotted a second sheet around the man's waist. With Sister John pulling and Sister Hyacinthe propping they succeeded in dragging him from the confines of the closet and across the floor to the mattress, after which Sister John knelt beside the man, cut away his shirt and began an appraisal of the damage.

"I believe he's been shot," she said at last.

"With a gun? In this house?" gasped Sister Hyacinthe.

"With a gun but not necessarily in this house because the wound's almost a day old. He's been shot three times and lost a great deal of blood, but the extraordinary thing is that none of the bullets stayed in him. It's really extraordinary."

"Why?" asked Sister Hyacinthe.

"Because it's a miracle," said Sister John impatiently. "One bullet grazed his scalp, a second tore his ear, while the third made this fiendish hole in the fleshy part of his arm but it went right through without touching anything vital. Just think, Sister Hyacinthe—three bullets and none of them killed him. Of course it's a miracle."

"Or someone who can't shoot straight."

"That too is a miracle," Sister John told her firmly.

The man's eyelids fluttered, a pair of glazed eyes opened to regard them blankly and Sister John leaned closer, speaking to him as if he were deaf. "You mustn't try to move, you're badly hurt," she shouted. "Just relax—we'll get a doctor for you, an ambulance and the police."

The man gave no evidence of relaxing; her words only appeared to agitate him. "No," he said, and then with a gasp, "No doctor, no amb—"

"Quiet," Sister John told him sharply. "You've simply got to have a doctor, you've lost a great deal of blood and if you'll just—"

"No," he shouted. "Hide." He struggled to sit up while Sister Hyacinthe held him down. "Sanctuary," he gasped. "I beg—sanctuary!" With that he collapsed into unconsciousness again.

"Sanctuary," murmured Sister John, looking pleased. "A religious man, wouldn't you say, Sister Hyacinthe?"

"Or a hunted one," put in Sister Hyacinthe indignantly. "We'll both be murdered in our beds tonight."

"Certainly not by him, and I don't think he was shot here," said Sister John, pointing, "because look at the trail of bloodstains going out the door. Sister Hyacinthe, it's a grave responsibility, sanctuary. Is there a chance of healing this man without a doctor?"

"You mean keep him *here*?"

"Yes, keep him here and heal him. We're under God's laws, not man's, and this poor soul has appealed to us for help."

Sister Hyacinthe edged closer. "You're sure there are no bullets in him, it's just a matter of—of holes?"

"Yes."

Sister Hyacinthe nodded. "I can try, at least until morning. When I was picking *Scutellaria lateriflora* on the thruway I put a puffball in my basket."

"Puffball," said Sister John blankly. "What else will you need?"

"More puffballs, probably, they stanch the bleeding. A comfrey poultice, too, but I brought comfrey and powdered slippery elm with me. Did we bring along any of Sister Elizabeth's dandelion wine?"

"She insisted."

Sister Hyacinthe brightened. "Considering the potency of Sister Elizabeth's dandelion wine, his chances increase."

They went down to the kitchen where Sister John unwrapped the bottle of wine from her bedroll. A sheet was torn up for bandages, and Sister Hyacinthe rummaged in her pack for dried herbs. She made a paste out of boiling water and powdered slippery elm bark, worked powdered comfrey root into it and spread the mixture, still hot, on a bandage. After this they went upstairs, carrying their odd paraphernalia on a tray. The

man barely stirred as Sister John scrubbed the caked
blood from his arm. When she had cleaned the wound
as best she could Sister Hyacinthe knelt beside the man,
crushed the puffball over the unpleasant hole in his arm
and carefully wrapped the warm comfrey poultice
around the arm.

"What do these things *do*?" asked Sister John anxiously.

"Pour the wine into the spoon, will you? Puffballs are
fungi, the only fungi the Indians ever trusted—the
spores clot the blood—comfrey has allantoin in it."

"How very astonishing," said Sister John, and knelt
beside their patient with her offering of wine. He
coughed, he weakly gagged but the wine went down his
throat. Sister John recorked the bottle and tucked a
blanket around him.

"Now," said Sister Hyacinthe, "there's nothing to do
but wait."

"And pray," pointed out Sister John. "Is he quite
comfortable?"

"A little fresh air, perhaps," said Sister Hyacinthe,
going to the window and opening it several inches. "A
teaspoon of wine every hour. The other wounds are
only scratches, they can be treated later. Leave the door
open, Sister John, so we can hear him if he calls out."

"We've missed Lauds and now Vespers and we can
only hope for Compline," said Sister John as they descended the wide, curving staircase. "I wonder who he
can be."

"I wonder who shot him," said Sister Hyacinthe.

"I don't suppose this is a deer-hunting season by any
chance?"

"No—no, I'm sure it's not the deer-hunting season."

"Then he was mugged," Sister John said, nodding.

"What exactly *is* mugging?"

"I've no idea but Mr. Armisbruck said it happens all the time these days, and is quite harmful. Have you noticed the drops of blood we're following? He came up these stairs not too many hours ago. That must have been when you saw him in a window. It will be interesting to see where these stains of blood lead."

It wasn't difficult to follow the man's route once the flashlight was concentrated on the floor. A consistent trail of dark spots led into the dining room past a large oak banquet table to the base of a french window where shards of glass lay on the floor. A small pane had been broken, a hand pushed through and the lock released from the inside. "At least he wasn't shot in the house, he stumbled inside," said Sister John.

The window was still ajar, tendrils of ivy curling around the knob. Sister John pushed the window wide and peered through a jungle of growth. "More bloodstains, Sister Hyacinthe. I think we should follow them and see where they come from. Bring the flashlight."

"What we really need is a machete," grumbled Sister Hyacinthe, following her.

They emerged on the open side porch and followed drops of blood down stairs to an earthen path where they lost the trail but picked it up some steps later on the bricked path in the rear. Passing the well and the birdbath, they left the privet hedge behind and emerged on the opposite side of the house, near the barn. Here stood a short, glass-windowed porch, latticed underneath; the blood led under the porch where the latticework had broken away. "He crept in underneath," said Sister Hyacinthe, dropping to her hands and knees.

"The dead leaves are still red." She dug up a handful of dirt and scattered it across the stains, obliterating them.

There was nothing more; from what direction the man had approached the hiding place it was impossible to guess because any other traces had been swallowed up by high grass and, as Sister John pointed out, he might not have begun to bleed until he crawled under the porch. They strolled toward the barn and to their surprise discovered a road behind the barn that entered the property from another point on Fallen Stump Road.

"And much more used, too," added Sister Hyacinthe, pointing to wheel marks baked into the earth by the hot sun. "This must have been the service entrance. Sister John, you're looking funny again."

"I'm thinking of fireworks. Didn't that extraordinary young man with the beard mention noises last night in the woods? We have a man upstairs with three bullet wounds in him, and he must have been shot nearby. He certainly couldn't have walked far." She stood in the middle of the dirt road, frowning. "It's quite possible. From here to that little porch is about two hundred yards. If the person who shot our patient stood about here on this road—and if it was quite dark—it would explain how our patient was able to get away. There's all that tall grass beside the road, and the privet hedge on the right. But it would have had to be dark, and they said it was dark when they heard the fireworks."

Sister Hyacinthe looked at her accusingly. "Sister John, you're enjoying this!"

"I used to adore crossword puzzles," confessed Sister John. "Let's have a look in the barn, it won't take but a moment."

Sister Hyacinthe sighed. "I've driven several hundred

miles today, Sister John, I've pulled money out of a well and a bleeding man out of a closet and we've still not had our supper."

Sister John absently patted her arm. "Just a glance," she promised, and strode across the lawn, skirts flying. But the barn, once she had encouraged the lock to snap, turned out to be empty of all but the usual barn accessories: a pitchfork, a scythe, several large empty oil drums, and a wall hung with old license plates. Sister John was forced to forego any new pleasures and return to the house.

Across the valley the sun lingered at the horizon, a fuzzy luminous red orb promising more heat tomorrow. They carried cheese and bread and tea to the front steps to watch the sunset—"Just like going to the theater," said Sister John—and to be efficient she brought writing paper and pencil with her because, she pointed out, the sisters of St. Tabitha would all be waiting anxiously to hear from them.

"In fact," she said, nibbling her pencil, "so anxiously that perhaps it might be a little too stimulating to tell them tonight about the man in the closet."

"It could be," conceded Sister Hyacinthe, stirring her tea.

Leaning over the writing tablet Sister John began her letter. *Dear Mother Angelique and Sisters,* she wrote. *Rest in the heart of Christ, we have arrived safely. The Moretti house is large—once very grand—and full of unexpected surprises. We have been unnaturally busy, about which I will write tomorrow. Pray for us. Yours in Christ, Sister John.*

"You haven't told them about the money, either," pointed out Sister Hyacinthe.

"No," admitted Sister John, "but I'll tuck a twenty-dollar bill inside and explain tomorrow." Her eyes moved across the valley to the setting sun. "St. Tabitha's tonight seems a most blessed place, Sister Hyacinthe. There feels very little nourishment in this world we've entered. Shall we say a prayer for it now?"

They knelt on the steps and prayed for their sisters at St. Tabitha's, for peace in the world, for the poor and the sick and for the stranger in the room upstairs. They locked up the house and spread their bedrolls in the hall upstairs so that they could give their patient a teaspoonful of dandelion wine every hour and hear him if he called out. After briefly meditating they lay down on their bedrolls.

Sister Hyacinthe suddenly began to giggle.

"What on earth," said Sister John.

"I'm so thirsty, Sister John. I was thinking of the verse of a psalm that begins, 'In a desert and pathless land where no water is . . .' Do you think we'll find water tomorrow?"

"Go to sleep," Sister John told her firmly.

3

Sometime during the night it began to thunder and Sister John woke up, marveling at finding herself on the floor of a mansion instead of asleep in her cell at St. Tabitha's. The thunder was low and growling and the wind rising, setting all the vines to work downstairs tapping at the windows. Sister John climbed out of her bedroll and went into the small room where their patient lay. She turned on the flashlight as she entered and glanced at her wrist watch. It was three o'clock in the morning.

"Put out the flashlight!" hissed Sister Hyacinthe from the window.

"Whatever are you doing there?" asked Sister John, flicking off the torch.

"Come and see for yourself."

The man at Sister John's feet was snoring gently; considering Sister Elizabeth's dandelion wine she thought he might be in a state of mild inebriation but at least he was still alive. She moved to the window and stood beside Sister Hyacinthe and thought for a moment that she was witnessing a phenomenon of fireflies invading the rear garden. She counted five small lights.

"There are three men with flashlights down there," whispered Sister Hyacinthe.

"I count five."

"Two of the lights are the parking lights of a car."

She was quite right of course; only three of the lights danced and bobbed across the ground, attached to human hands, no doubt, which placed the scene on a less supernatural level.

"They have no right," murmured Sister John, and then, "That's enough of that!" Before Sister Hyacinthe could stop her she opened the window wider and leaned out into the rain. "What are you doing here?" she called.

Her voice blended with a particularly loud crack of thunder—the storm was very near—and she was forced to repeat her words. "What," she shouted, "are you doing on this property?" A bolt of lightning accompanied her second attempt and illuminated the garden like noonday. Three men in white belted raincoats stopped and stared up at her in dumbfounded astonishment, the rain pelting their faces, eyes blinking. The nearest and largest man stood just below them: his was a flat round face, made somewhat less attractive by his mouth being open.

He stared at Sister John in the window and said, "What the—" Thunder censored his exclamation and then as he added, *"—dames?"* the lightning vanished and the darkness turned stygian.

"I can't see them, what are they doing now?" asked Sister John.

Sister Hyacinthe, who could see in the dark like a

cat, said, "They're moving to the car, Sister John, you've put them to the run."

"They looked very official but they didn't explain why they were trespassing."

"I don't think we could expect them to."

The men had grouped themselves around the car and appeared to be arguing. The murmur of voices rose, followed by an abrupt slamming of doors, the starting of the engine, and the slip-slap of wheels in mud. The parking lights moved slowly backward, the car turned, two red lights replaced the amber ones and the car vanished.

Sister Hyacinthe said, "They arrived about five minutes ago. They seemed particularly interested in looking under the porch."

Sister John said thoughtfully, "You may be right, Sister Hyacinthe, someone may very well have evil intentions toward this poor man on the floor. I don't *want* to think you were right—"

"I know that, Sister John."

"—but perhaps, having promised him sanctuary, we should take precautions." She turned on the flashlight and stared at the man on the mattress. "I think if the occasion arises we could say that a third sister has arrived from St. Tabitha's. We'll call him Sister Ursula."

"Call him *what*?"

"I don't see why not," reasoned Sister John. "It's only a very small rearrangement of the truth for compassionate purposes. He arrived from St. Tabitha's during the storm and he caught cold."

"You mean she caught a cold."

"Yes, of course, and has taken to her bed. His pulse is almost normal," she said, her fingers on his wrist.

"How many teaspoons of dandelion wine have you given him, Sister Hyacinthe?"

"Six."

"Good heavens, I've given him seven. That's thirteen—it should be enough for the night."

"Unless we've embalmed him," said Sister Hyacinthe.

"Oh, I don't think the alcohol content is that high. Almost but not quite, although I daresay eggnog would be a pleasant change for him tomorrow. Those two young campers said they had eggs, didn't they? We'll go and see them first thing in the morning."

"Yes," said Sister Hyacinthe, yawning, "Can we go back to bed now?"

"Of course." They groped their way back to the bedrolls in the hall. "I don't like the idea of leaving our patient alone for long, but if we go early enough—one must assume that even evil sleeps sometime."

"Sleep," murmured Sister Hyacinthe longingly.

"In any case all this rain is washing away the blood outside. By the way, I took a closer look at that man's face—our patient's, I mean—and I thought it infinitely superior to the face of the man I saw under the window, even with his eyes closed. His chin is better. That's reassuring, don't you think?"

But there was no reply from Sister Hyacinthe.

In the morning, after Matins and breakfast, they set out for the woods behind the garden, carefully locking both the van and the house before leaving. It was a beautiful day, fresh with scents of wet earth and growing things, the birds tugging at worms in the garden and splashing in puddles of rainwater. Sister Hyacinthe carried a basket into which she hoped to put plants for lunch and dinner, and Sister John carried a loaf of bread. Since the bearded young man named Brill had found them by way of the path through the woods, they hoped that the path would in turn lead them straight to his camp. Sister Hyacinthe, however, was incapable of following a straight line, and once she discovered borage growing near the edge of the wood Sister John knew there would be no hurrying her. Deeper in the wood the moss was thick and springy under their feet. There were also damp, decaying leaves—"mulch!" cried Sister Hyacinthe ecstatically—and when they encountered fiddlehead ferns and stalks of mullein her gasps grew more pronounced and her steps slower.

Presently she moved from the narrow path into a clump of bushes and only her head could be seen as she bent over. "I've found another puffball," she called back to Sister John. "There's peppermint here, too—*Mentha piperita*—and more mullein, and I do believe—" She broke off at the sound of twigs snapping under heavy feet nearby. Sister John, waiting patiently on the path, heard the noise too, and looked toward the clearing ahead.

A man emerged from a thicket and without looking to right or left walked very quickly across their line of vision. He was dressed in a dark suit, a white shirt and black tie, but the effect was marred by the soiled plastic sack that he carried over one shoulder. Just as he reached the center of the clearing—Sister John was debating whether she ought to call out "Good Morning"—a child of seven or eight appeared at the edge of the wood behind the man. There were two details about the boy that astonished Sister John: he was

carrying a bow and arrow which he proceeded to lift
and aim at the man, and he wore no clothes at all. He
was completely and unabashedly naked.

The drawstring of the bow twanged faintly and an arrow shot across the clearing, plunged into the man's
sack, and hung there, quivering. Sister John, for reasons
she later found difficult to understand, ducked her head.
When she lifted it the clearing was deserted; both man
and boy had disappeared.

"What an incredible thing to see!" gasped Sister
John. "If I described what I saw to anyone they'd think
me mad. I did see it, didn't I?"

"Of course you did, it was a bull's-eye."

Sister John felt that a bull's-eye was the least extraordinary thing about the child but she ignored this.
"Which of them should we make inquiries of? Surely
no one was hurt?"

"I think," said Sister Hyacinthe, "that the man only
lost his sack but the child had lost his clothes."

Sister John nodded. "He took this path?"

"Yes, next to the alders."

They plunged into the underbrush again and redis-
covered the path, a traveled one now of hard beaten
earth. They caught a glimpse of the boy at some distance ahead and quickened their steps. He broke into a
run, and so did Sister John and Sister Hyacinthe, so that
when they reached the next clearing they were in full
gallop and their sudden stop was disorderly.

This clearing was occupied by a bright blue
Volkswagen bus with flowers painted all over its back,
sides, front, roof and hood. Behind it, in a sunny tree-
less patch of land, lay a neatly tended vegetable garden;
a line of rope between two birches bore a row of drying

blue jeans; and in the foreground stood a primitive fireplace of rocks. Around this fireplace sat four people cross-legged, their eyes closed and a sound emanating from them like that of bees buzzing in a flower. One of them was Brill, another, Naomi. "Ommmmm," they murmured in unison, and then the naked child flew out of the bushes, three startled hens scuttled across the camp, clucking and scolding noisily, and four pairs of eyes opened and stared at Sisters John and Hyacinthe.

"Good morning," Sister John said breathlessly. "I wonder if you've noticed that your little boy has no clothes on."

This news seemed to have little effect; four pairs of eyes regarded them without expression until Naomi abruptly uncrossed her legs and smiled. "That's Ché," she said. "We washed his jeans for him last night, he doesn't have any other clothes. He's not ours, he's with the migrant workers up the road."

"He shot a man with his bow and arrow," Sister Hyacinthe said eagerly. "A man carrying a plastic bag."

"Quigley, of course," said Brill, rising. "Did Ché hit him?"

"He hit the bag."

Brill nodded. "That was our garbage in the bag, he collects it."

"Then he's the garbage man," said Sister John. "And Ché doesn't like him?"

The girl with long black braids and freckles stood up and brushed off her pants. "We all *try* to like Quigley," she said. "We don't really have any garbage because we use it for compost, but we collect things for him and pretend not to notice when he takes them. We give him our *Rolling Stone*s and Los Angeles *Free Press*es, and we put in notes saying we love him. He must hate that," she added.

Neither Sister John nor Sister Hyacinthe knew what she was talking about, but the child was climbing into a pair of ragged shorts and if Mr. Quigley was a garbage collector, however well dressed, he was perhaps accustomed, like postmen, to barking dogs and hostile children. "We brought you a loaf of abbey bread and wondered if we could buy an egg," said Sister John.

"Have we an egg?" asked the long thin young man.

"This is Alfie," said Naomi. "Alfred Comstock Geer, and my friend here in braids is Sunrise."

"What a beautiful name," breathed Sister Hyacinthe.

"Actually she's Gloria Schlaughterbeck," explained Alfie, "but she's changing her identity for the summer."

"Just as we do in orders!" exclaimed Sister John. "In a manner of speaking, of course."

Sunrise said, "The nuns we know wear short skirts and no veils. Aren't you awfully hot in those clothes?"

"They must be the new nuns," Sister Hyacinthe said wistfully. "We've been in cloister, you see, until Mr. Moretti died and left the house to St. Tabitha's."

"Which means we're on their land," Brill told the others.

"We tried," said Alfie. "We asked neighbors who owned the land but nobody seemed to know."

"What's cloister? And what's in your basket?" asked Naomi.

"Cloister means we're a contemplative order living behind walls, and Sister Hyacinthe has herbs in her basket."

"Like what?" asked Sunrise, peering into it.

"Puffballs," said Sister Hyacinthe shyly. "And borage and mullein and peppermint—"

"What in the world do you *do* with them?"

"Well—borage is a beautiful vegetable, you cook it like spinach. Here, take some," said Sister Hyacinthe generously. "And mullein—"

"Greens?" said Alfie disbelievingly. "If that's a green vegetable give them two eggs for nothing. I'll make any sacrifice if it'll improve the menu, which," he said, looking intently at Sister Hyacinthe, "is mainly soybean until our own vegetables come up. Soybean, followed by more soybean, followed by soybean with eggs. Stay for breakfast, too."

"Oh, thank you but we couldn't stay. Another sister arrived last night—"

"Sister Ursula," added Sister Hyacinthe, bobbing her head.

"And she's caught cold—"

"—and is feeling poorly," finished Sister Hyacinthe with artistic flourish.

"In any case we haven't even found out yet how to turn the water on at the house. We have a busy day ahead of us."

"Alfie could turn on the water for you," said Brill, pulling on a sweat shirt. "Alfie's not working today."

"A joyful thought," said Alfie, looking interested. "Kinder than giving the bus a grease job, although I suppose you want me to do that, too?"

"Naturally. And weed the garden, feed the chickens, cook dinner and—"

"Where do you all work?" asked Sister John, puzzled.

"We're picking beans this week at the farm up the

road. We take turns. Three of us go, one stays at home
to keep house. Ché picks beans, too, don't you, Ché?"

The boy grinned as Brill ruffled his dark hair.

"Do you sleep on the bus?" asked Sister Hyacinthe,
who had been giving it admiring glances.

"Only when it rains," said Naomi, and brought her
two eggs, placing them gently in her basket. "We give
you two eggs and Alfie. Thanks for the bread, it'll be
great."

"About the firecrackers," began Sister John.

Four heads swiveled to look at her. "Firecrackers?"

"I was wondering if you could describe exactly what
you heard the other night. You mentioned firecrackers?"

"Bangs," said Brill briefly. "About five."

"But not all together," pointed out Sunrise.

"Two first," said Naomi. "Sharp noises, like cherry
bombs."

"I thought like two strings of firecrackers."

"Acoustics probably," said Alfie. "Noise carries at
night but it was enough to wake the dead. It woke *us*,
and we turn in at midnight. Why?"

Sister John turned pink. "I just wondered. Sister
Hyacinthe, we'd better be getting back since we have so
much to do."

"Wait for me, I'm giving you an hour of my priceless
time," said Alfie, shrugging into a shirt. "You don't
mind, do you? I mean, cloister nuns don't have to be
chaperoned, do they?"

Sister John laughed; she had a light, melodious laugh
that was a pleasure to hear. "Come along and don't talk
nonsense."

"And Alfie—when you get back," called Naomi,

"don't forget the leaflets, and if Peg-Leg stops in tell him about the meeting tonight."

"God," said Alfie.

"Oh, definitely," said Sister John, giving him a cheerful glance.

4

As they plunged along the path through the woods Sister John said, "What exactly brought you here to camp for the summer and pick beans? You're not Boy Scouts after all?"

Alfie looked startled. "No, we're not Boy Scouts. Actually we're working at Nothingness, we've given up worldly pleasures."

Both sisters stopped and stared at him. "Given up worldly pleasures!" said Sister John. "Are you in orders, too?"

Alfie grinned. "You might say we belong to the anti-Quigley back-to-the-earth movement, or you might just call us dropouts. Quigley would."

"This Quigley," began Sister John, but Alfie jumped up, seized the branch of a low-tree and swung on it, giving a Tarzan-like shout. "Let's not talk about Quigley," he said, dropping back to the path. "It's too gorgeous a day. I don't believe you live in a house at all, I think you're wood sprites. Show me your mystery house."

But when they emerged from the wood and he saw the house he looked stunned. "Wow," he said.

"What's the matter?"

"That's Gothic Revival. Haunted Gothic Revival." He dashed across the paths and knelt beside the foundation; when he stood up he looked ecstatic. "You've got a house here that's probably two hundred years old, did you know that? Part of it, anyway. Then about a hundred years ago somebody came along and added on to it, remodeled it and turned it into an authentic Gothic Revival. It's amazing. Does anybody know about your house, does anybody know it's here?"

"Mr. Moretti," said Sister John.

"And several other men," put in Sister Hyacinthe. "Where did you learn so much about houses?"

"I was an architect major until it began stunting my growth," explained Alfie. "Can I see the inside?"

"We're hoping you'll want to see the cellar," Sister Hyacinthe reminded him, "and find the water switch?"

"Oh, the cellar ought to be fantastically spooky."

"I think you can count on it."

"As you can see, the living room is strange enough," said Sister John, unlocking the front door and entering the main hall. "The vines have covered up all the windows and it's black as night."

"And the vines tap on the glass in a wind," added Sister Hyacinthe.

"Marvelous," breathed Alfie.

"The cellar door is over here," said Sister John, leading the way. "Perhaps you'd like a flashlight. Perhaps you'd like to go first in case there are rats. Sister Hyacinthe, could you give him the flashlight?"

Once Alfie was properly outfitted he began a slow

descent of the steep wooden stairs to the basement.
"Watch this third one," he called over his shoulder. "It
wobbles a bit but I can see a light bulb hanging near the
bottom of the stairs. No rats, not even a mouse, but lots
of cobwebs. I've got it," he said, tugging at a string suspended from the rafters, and a feeble low-watt bulb
spread a sickly glow over their faces.

"Oh dear," said Sister Hyacinthe, looking around her.

Cobwebs stretched like clotheslines from every rafter
and beam, and from their woolly threads hung newer,
more delicate webs, like embroidery. A massive wall of
ancient whitewashed stone ran down the center of the
cellar, with small wooden doors set into it at intervals.
There was only one window to be seen and it shed less
light than the ten-watt bulb above them. Between them
and the window lay a dark void filled with the silhou-
ettes of discarded furniture: old chairs, wooden barrels
and ladders.

"Very Poe," said Alfie in a hushed voice. "Can't you
hear the faint dying cries of men sealed into the walls?"

"Actually no," said Sister John calmly.

Alfie picked up a broom and began assaulting the
cobwebs. "Some of these old houses have ghosts, you
know, wouldn't it be great if yours had one, too?" Hearing a small sound from Sister Hyacinthe he turned and
looked at her.

"It's just that we have to sleep in the house, you
know."

"Oh." He thought about this and nodded. "You may
have a point there, although I can't think of anything
more fun. Imagine meeting a ghost face-to-face, think
of the conversation you could have with him. There's a

lot of money in haunted houses, too, you could charge admission—"

"About the water meter," began Sister John.

"Oh, that." Alfie said impatiently, "Well, there are the pipes up there, running down from your kitchen and along the ceiling. They head in this direction—" Swatting cobwebs, he moved up the aisle with Sisters John and Hyacinthe behind him and opened the door to the first room. It proved to be a storeroom filled with old furniture covered with holland cloths but in the corner behind a particularly thick nest of cobwebs Alfie found the water meter with its accompanying wheels and knobs. "It's very simple," he said. "Nobody ever switched on your water." He turned a valve, and the sound of water rushing into pipes brought smiles to the faces of Sister Hyacinthe and Sister John.

"How can we ever thank you?" said Sister John.

"No charge. But you can't stop exploring this terrific cellar now, can you? I mean, all these ancient mysterious rooms and they're yours?"

"Perhaps a quick look," said Sister John, exchanging glances with Sister Hyacinthe, "although we simply must make Sister Ursula some eggnog and carry it up to her soon."

They were presently indebted to Alfie for his persistence, however, because over half of the long center wall proved to be a wine cellar, partially stocked with bottles, and all of them looking, said Sister John, as if they might be worth some money if sold: she only wished that she had brought pencil and paper with her to inventory them. Three of the small doors opened into the dim wine cellars; the fourth door, at the end of the basement, proved to be a preserve closet.

"But empty," pointed out Sister John. "Such a pity."

Sister Hyacinthe, walking down the aisle between the shelves, said, "Not completely empty, Sister John, there's an oil painting up there in a gilt frame."

Alfie turned the flashlight on a charming portrait of a young girl seated on a garden bench, a great deal of pointed lace at her throat and long dark hair framing a piquant face. "She looks familiar," Sister Hyacinthe said, frowning over it.

"I do believe ... Sister Hyacinthe, do you remember Sister Emma, who died the same week as Mother Clothilde? Do you remember what she looked like?"

Standing on tiptoe, Sister John reached for the painting and accidentally knocked the shelf with her elbow. The shelf collapsed, sending the portrait to the floor in a cloud of dust and alarming a nest of mice below. As the mice raced across the room emitting small squeaks of anguish, Sister Hyacinthe choked back a cry and backed hard against the wall, which precipitated a hollow rumbling sound. Slowly, majestically, the narrow wall of shelves behind her began to move, and like a revolving door carried Sister Hyacinthe away with it.

"She's vanished!" gasped Alfie.

Sister John sighed. "This sort of thing is *so* upsetting for Sister Hyacinthe."

"But she's found a secret room!" cried Alfie. "Do you realize the odds against ever finding one by accident? A person could take measurements of the house for days, weeks, months and never know it was here!"

"Nevertheless," said Sister John firmly, "you simply must bring her back."

But the rumbling had resumed and a moment later Sister Hyacinthe was returned to them covered with dust, her coif askew. She said unsteadily, "One can't even lean against a wall in this house. Sister John, I thought I'd never see you again."

"What's back there?" demanded Alfie.

She turned and gave him a brooding stare. "I daresay you'll be disappointed to hear there wasn't a single body there, not so much as a skeleton. Only steep narrow stairs."

"A secret staircase! Oh, even better!" gasped Alfie. "Come on, what are we waiting for?"

"For someone to be sensible and leave this house of horrors," said Sister Hyacinthe.

"I confess to some curiosity," admitted Sister John. "Sister Hyacinthe—"

Sister Hyacinthe sighed. "I knew you'd say that. One thing leads to another in the place, except I *thought* it would lead to eggnog."

"Soon," promised Sister John, and volunteered to go first.

One by one they pushed hard against the wall, which swung inward, circling past a blank wall to deposit them at the foot of narrow wooden stairs. When they had assembled, each on a step, Alfie led the way, attacking the cobwebs with his broom, and Sister John in the rear with the flashlight. One wall was stone, and dripped moisture; the other was paneled and gray with mildew. Up they went, losing all sense of distance and space, and when it seemed as if they must surely have reached the roof Alfie hit something and swore. "I've come to the end, my nose reached it first, damn it. There's nowhere left to go." He grunted, pushed and tugged. "Something's sliding," he said, and abruptly the darkness became less intense and a strong smell of mothballs assailed their nostrils. "I think I'm in a closet," Alfie called over his shoulder. A door opened and beyond Alfie's silhouette they saw light and heard him gasp, *"Good God!"*

Sister Hyacinthe turned and looked at Sister John in alarm. Hastily the two sisters climbed over the last step and hurried through the closet to find themselves in the room over the kitchen. Alfie was standing over the man on the mattress and staring down at him incredulously.

"Oh dear, you're not supposed to see him," said Sister John. "That's Sister Ursula."

"This is Sister Ursula?"

"Not really, of course," put in Sister Hyacinthe, "but we're trying to call him that to hide his being here. Sister John, have you noticed he's moved? He's lying on his side now."

"A very healthy sign," agreed Sister John.

"But why?" asked Alfie, looking shaken. "I mean, who is he and what's he doing lying on your floor? Did you bring him with you?"

"Oh no, he came with the house," said Sister John.

Alfie's jaw dropped. "You mean like a stove or refrigerator?"

"You could say that. We found him unconscious in the closet and we think he's in danger because he asked for sanctuary."

"You've got to be kidding, why should he be in danger?"

"Because he's been shot three times. With bullets."

Alfie stared at her blankly. "With bullets," he echoed, and a look of comprehension suddenly dawned on his face. "He was here when you got here yesterday and he'd been shot three times?" He snapped his fingers.

"The fireworks! That's why you asked about the fireworks, something *did* happen here two nights ago!"

"You're very quick."

"It's my IQ," he said modestly. "It's 160."

"All that meat," pointed out Sister Hyacinthe, nodding. "They were feeding meat to new babies when I went into orders and I wondered how it would turn out."

With a glance at the man on the floor between them Sister John put a finger to her lips and gestured them toward the door. "Let's continue our talk in the kitchen while I make eggnog, our voices are loud."

"Yes, but who do you think he is?" asked Alfie. "Where did he come from? Why d'ye suppose he was shot?"

"I think we shall have to wait for him to grow well enough to tell us."

"With three bullets in him you're going to just *wait*?"

"I see no alternative," Sister John told him as she led them down the stairs. "In the meantime there seem to be a number of equally pressing matters to look into. That portrait in the preserve closet, for one thing. That *was* a portrait of Sister Emma," she said, turning to Sister Hyacinthe. "A much younger Sister Emma, of course, but you recognized something familiar at once. If St. Tabitha's Abbey and Mr. Moretti are fatally linked to one another I think we ought to know how. His lawyer wouldn't even tell us whether Mr. Moretti died in a state of grace or not."

"But Mr. Moretti's dead," protested Alfie, "while upstairs you've got a living, breathing mystery man."

"Nevertheless I like to begin at the beginning," said Sister John. "I like a firm base."

"Something you can get your teeth into?"

"Exactly. A sense of order, a stable background in which to place events, which I must say appear to be accumulating rapidly. I like to see how things work."

"Sister John fixes all the machinery at St. Tabitha's," Sister Hyacinthe told him shyly. "She knows how to put everything in order."

"That's all very well but that chap upstairs can't have anything to do with machines and putting things in order."

"What we're speaking of," said Sister John gently, "is divine order." She picked up one of the two eggs on the table and cracked it over a bowl. "Have you the powdered milk there, Sister Hyacinthe?"

Alfie watched dazedly as an egg beater and powdered milk were produced. "But aren't you *worried*? I mean, if he was shot in this house—"

"He wasn't, he came in through the dining-room window. You can look for yourself if you'd like."

"Thanks." Alfie headed for the dining room and returned a minute later looking thoughtful. "I wonder if you'd mind my mentioning your Sister Ursula chap to the others. Brill and Naomi and Sunrise, I mean. I hate keeping secrets."

"Can they?"

"Oh yes, and we all might be able to help, too. For instance, we can start by repairing that broken window for you. But I'd still like to know what you plan to do about that guy upstairs."

"We plan to give him eggnog."

"When he could be a murderer or worse?"

"There's a good deal to be said for letting God judge such matters," Sister John told him serenely, "and His are the rules we live by here. Sister Hyacinthe, would you take the eggnog upstairs? I'm going to turn on the faucets very gently and make sure the pressure doesn't break the pipes."

Alfie sighed. "I can take a hint if it's broad enough. I'll leave you, then, but I'm going to stop in later if you don't mind."

"To make sure we've not been murdered," Sister Hyacinthe said approvingly.

"Not necessarily by your Sister Ursula, either," he reminded her. "My deduction is simple: whoever shot your Sister Ursula wanted him dead, at least three bullets implies a certain—a certain—"

"Sincerity?" suggested Sister Hyacinthe.

"Yes, as well as three miscalculations. Whoever shot him may have doubts about his success and come back to make sure there's a body."

"An interesting deduction," agreed Sister John.

He glanced at his watch. "Good God, half-past nine already?" With a wave of his hand Alfie bolted out of the kitchen door, returned to gasp, "Don't let anybody in!" and left.

Sister Hyacinthe said accusingly, "You heard what he said."

"His deductions are shrewd but late," Sister John said calmly, "or have you forgotten the men in the garden last night?" She carefully turned on the faucet and stood back as water exploded into the sink. Pipes rattled and shuddered, and water settled into a quiet stream and she nodded in satisfaction. "It's working properly now. I'll go upstairs with you."

When they entered the room over the kitchen their patient's eyes were wide open and staring at the ceiling;

he closed them quickly. Sister Hyacinthe said, "I've brought you eggnog and I know you're awake so you needn't play games. How are you feeling this morning?"

"Awful," he said, opening his eyes and staring at her. "Who are you?"

"I'm Sister Hyacinthe, this is Sister John, and we'd like to know who *you* are."

"It's none of your business."

"If you hadn't been our business yesterday," Sister Hyacinthe said tartly, "we would have left you in the closet to bleed to death, so you can at least be civil. Sit up and drink this eggnog."

He dug his elbows into the mattress, tried to lift himself and sank back. "Christ, I'm weak as a kitten," he gasped.

"And if you take the name of the Lord in vain He won't bother to come around when you really need Him. I'll prop up your shoulders—so—and tilt the glass. Now sip."

When an inch of the eggnog had disappeared she lowered him, loosened his bandage, sniffed the wound and nodded. "There's no infection or gangrene, Sister John, I think he's beginning to heal. I'll make a fresh poultice for him tonight."

Sister John, adjusting the curtain at the window, said over her shoulder, "Is there someone you'd like us to notify? A wife, your family, children?"

He shook his head. "Nobody to notify. I'm dead."

Sister Hyacinthe said hopefully. "Then is there anybody we can notify of your death?"

"Very f-f-funny."

"Not really," said Sister John, moving across the

room to face him. "Of course you're not yourself today—whoever that is—but I'd like to remind you that you asked sanctuary of us last night. If you want us to keep hiding you then a few questions seem reasonable. It's a matter of conscience."

"Oh God," he groaned.

Her glance was stern. "Are you a mugger?"

"A what?"

"Mugger."

Looking dazed, he shook his head.

"Have you killed someone?"

This appeared to galvanize him. "Certainly not," he said in an aggrieved voice. "Look, for God's sake hide me for a few days, don't turn me out."

"We're already hiding you."

"But if anyone comes asking, you won't tell them I'm here?"

"Oh, we can't lie," Sister John told him reproachfully.

"Absolutely not," said Sister Hyacinthe behind her.

"We can, however, tell anyone who asks that Sister Ursula is upstairs," she continued. "That wouldn't be a lie—that is, if you don't mind being Sister Ursula."

"Who?" he said, puzzled.

"You."

"I don't think he understands," Sister Hyacinthe told her. "It's a little tricky for him to catch right now. It's a little tricky for me, too."

Sister John nodded. "Then I'll just measure him. I'm going to take your measurements," she told the man in a loud voice. "Just lie quietly and don't be alarmed."

"Measurements?" he said blankly. "For what, a shroud?"

"Lie still. After I've measured him, Sister Hyacinthe, I think we'll have to make a very quick trip into Gatesville in the van."

"But why?"

"To mail our letter to St. Tabitha's and buy a little meat for our patient, among other things."

"What other things?" asked Sister Hyacinthe suspiciously. "We can't keep leaving Sister Ursula alone. Look at him, he's fallen asleep again, the man's completely defenseless."

Sister John sighed. "I suppose you're right. It's a nuisance but we'll have to open the door to Alfie's secret passage and slip him inside. I think there's room on the landing for the mattress—there may not be much air but there's space. We'll make it a very quick trip to Gatesville."

"You know I'm tired of driving," burst out Sister Hyacinthe, "and we were going to do such *nice* things this morning."

"We'll do them this afternoon," Sister John told her ruthlessly. "You and I have some detective work to do."

"I don't like this," complained Sister Hyacinthe as they headed toward Gatesville. "That was a very damp place to leave Sister Ursula, and it's not like you to be so unfeeling."

"I promised you a *very* quick trip," said Sister John. "We'll go first to the Town Hall, I think. I saw it on the main street yesterday when we drove past."

"Why there?"

"I want to find out how long Mr. Moretti owned this property, I want to know when he bought it and how long the house has been empty. Trust me, Sister Hyacinthe."

They pulled up at the court house behind a car whose rear bumper carried a sticker saying SISTERHOOD IS BEAUTIFUL. Sister Hyacinthe nudged her companion and pointed. "Nuns."

"No—no, I don't think so," said Sister John in astonishment as two young girls in bikinis climbed out of the car and strolled toward the main street.

Sister Hyacinthe, blushing for them, said, "What can it mean?"

"We'll ask Alfie," Sister John told her in a puzzled voice. "Obviously there are a great many things we don't understand yet but we can learn, Sister Hyacinthe." She lifted her skirts and climbed out of the van, and a few minutes later they were confronting a pleasant, freckle-faced young clerk at the tax desk. Sister John explained their mission.

"Fallen Stump Road?" echoed the girl, and moving to a filing cabinet, she brought back a drawer, placed it on the counter and removed a card. "We've had notice the property has been left to a St. Tabitha's Abbey—" Her glance lifted to Sister John's habit and she grinned. "Is that you?"

"In a manner of speaking," said Sister John. "Can you tell us something about Mr. Moretti?"

"About him?" The girl looked puzzled. "Well, I can only look up the old records. I've never met him, I don't think anybody ever met him. I know his tax payments came on time because I handled them myself. Just a minute, I'll look in the back."

She returned wearing glasses that slid down her nose as she frowned over a long sheet of foolscap. "Here we

are," she said. "The property was purchased in late
1953 from the Hathaway estate by Joseph Alfred
Moretti of Morningside Drive, New York City. Let's
see, assessments, easements . . . He must have been living in the house, or planning to live there, because a
building permit was issued in early 1954 for a new
wing containing kitchen, bathrooms, nursery and a rec-
reation room."

"I hope not in Gothic Revival," murmured Sister
John.

"But it was never built," continued the girl, "or so a
note explains that's attached here, so of course we never
taxed him for it. After that—" She put down the paper
and peered in the file drawer. "After 1955 he abandoned
the place, apparently, and his billing address changed
from Morningside Drive to an address in the East
Eighties in Manhattan, and then in 1959 he moved to
Miami Beach, Florida, and then in 1963, he moved
again for a last time."

"Could we have that last address?" asked Sister John.

"Yes, it's in care of Cherpin, Holtz, Smith, and Bar-
ney, Attorneys-at-law, Park Avenue, New York."

Sister John sighed. "Which brings us full circle back
to Mr. Samuel Cherpin, who refuses to tell us anything
at all." She nodded absently to the girl. "You've been
very informative. Thank you."

She grinned. "Yes I have, considering the property
will be non-taxable if you people move in. Is that all?"

"That's all," said Sister John.

"Well, I don't know what you learned," grumbled
Sister Hyacinthe as they walked out of the office, "but
it took ten minutes, Sister John."

"But isn't it fun?" asked Sister John, looking pleased.

"And it's not at all true that we learned nothing. One," she said, holding up a finger, "Mr. Moretti was restless—think of all those moves, Sister Hyacinthe! Two, he was a very sentimental man to keep the house all those years. Three, he was very secretive. And," she went on eagerly, "there could be a link with St. Tabitha's because did you notice that he changed his mind about living in the house the very same year that St. Tabitha's Abbey was established?"

Sister Hyacinthe looked at her radiant face and felt a stab of foreboding. "Sister John, we're not detectives, we're nuns."

Sister John brushed this aside impatiently. "If we can grow vegetables and print a newspaper and raise goats and live in the presence of God, and bake bread and butcher a cow I don't see why we can't solve a few finite mysteries as well, Sister Hyacinthe. Now do let's stop talking; think of Sister Ursula in the closet."

"Oh dear yes," gasped Sister Hyacinthe.

"To save time I think we can divide the remaining errands. You take the grocery store and I'll just step into the fabric shop. I want to buy five yards of blue cotton."

"Is that why you—You can't be serious, Sister John! You wouldn't dare."

"I'm thinking of chameleons," said Sister John. "They take on the color of their surroundings, they vanish into the scenery. We have a conspicuous man to hide, Sister Hyacinthe—any man staying in a house with nuns is conspicuous—and our patient can't vanish into the scenery. We can't turn him into a tree and it's not healthy for him to hide very long in that secret passage, but I see no reason why we can't turn him into a nun."

"It's sacrilegious, Sister John!"

"Nonsense, I'm sure it isn't. Besides," she concluded, "It isn't going to be a real habit, it only needs to look like one from a distance. Pope *John* would have understood, I'm sure of it, God rest his soul."

Sister Hyacinthe sighed. "You have such perfect faith, Sister John."

5

Sister Ursula was retrieved from the secret passage, given a shot of dandelion wine to revive him and a cup of valerian tea to tranquilize him. Into the soup kettle went stew beef to simmer and to send out ambrosial fumes once thyme and sage, onion, basil and tarragon had been joined to it. Following this they began their serious work, Sister Hyacinthe standing on a ladder outside the living room cutting ivy from the windows, Sister John inside the living room removing dust cloths and making a list of the furniture that appeared. Once a single window had been cleared of vines it became possible to open the window and call back and forth, and it was in this manner that Sister Hyacinthe learned a piano was being unwrapped that was nothing less than a Boysendorfer, that there was an old-fashioned wind-up Victrola in a cabinet, a number of slip-seat mahogany chairs, a Victorian cherrywood sofa, a charming *prie-dieu*, and some rather bad paintings in gilt frames.

None of this meant anything to Sister Hyacinthe, who in turn called to Sister John that the wisteria was dying from lack of pruning, that if she could only sickle the

huge front lawn it would yield enough mustard for a
dozen years of mustard plasters, and there was a robin's
nest under the porch eaves. She was still on the stepladder when a crunch of gravel met her ears and, knowing
that Sister John was in the living room, she turned and
saw a young man walking around the side of the barn
from the service entrance driveway. He was a vision of
sartorial splendor, cool and fresh in a striped summer
suit, hair soothingly short and pomaded, his wine-
colored shirt and tie exquisitely matched. Under one
arm he carried a clipboard. When he saw Sister
Hyacinthe his steps slackened and a peculiar expression
of dismay crossed his face. His glance took in the skirt
of her habit and jumped to her veil; he narrowed his
eyes as if he were nearsighted and couldn't trust his vision. *"A nun?"* he said in a shocked voice.

From the window Sister John said, "We're both
nuns."

"Two nuns," he said, and squinted into the vines in
search of the second voice. "I had no idea. Nobody told
me. That is, that we had new sisters in Gatesville."
Having survived the shock his voice rallied and grew
heartier. "Welcome, welcome. You've met Father Daniel in town?"

Sister Hyacinthe shook her head, awed by his immac-
ulateness; even the crease of his pants looked sharp
enough to slice a hair. "Are you looking for someone?"

"For *you*," he said, flashing a dazzling smile composed of bright square teeth and muscular cheeks. "I'm
taking the town census, Sister, the Gatesville census. I
hope you can spare a moment for a few questions?" He
lifted his clipboard, brought out a pen, and placed one

black boot on the bottom rung of the stepladder. "May I ask how many rooms in this house?"

"Nine," said Sister Hyacinthe.

"Ten," said Sister John from the window.

"Ten," he murmured, bending over his clipboard. "Running water?"

"Today, yes."

"Number of bathrooms?"

"Two."

"Thank you, And now," he added carefully, "how many people are living in this house?"

"Three," replied Sister John. "May we ask what your name is?"

"Name? Oh, Giovianni," he said, and put his pen back in his pocket and flashed a smile at them. "I don't have to ask your occupations, Sister, since I know it's putting in a good word for us sinners when you speak to God, but frankly I'm surprised to find nuns here. Could I ask what—uh—brings you to this house?"

"Are you Catholic, Mr. Giovianni?" asked Sister John from the window.

Startled, Mr. Giovianni said, "Baptized one, Sister, but may I ask what you're doing—"

"And have you been to Confession lately?"

Mr. Giovianni's smile caught in his teeth and turned garish, like a neon sign that had blown a fuse. "Confession? Well I can't say . . . that is—"

"Communion?"

Mr. Giovianni began to look alarmed. "Actually, Sister, I—that is I'm not—" He stopped and pulled himself together. "Actually," he said with dignity, "I think I have all the information I need now, Sister—ten rooms, two baths and three nuns in the house—and I don't think I should take up any more of your time, seeing how busy you are." He gave Sister Hyacinthe a brilliant smile. "Have a good day, both of you." He turned and walked rather quickly down the driveway.

"Nice young man," said Sister John, watching him go.

"Tidy," said Sister Hyacinthe.

"Very tidy," said Sister John, "but I'm afraid a fallen Catholic, Sister Hyacinthe. I think it's obvious that he's strayed from God, I only hope I succeeded in touching his conscience."

"You certainly touched something because he left in a great hurry," said Sister Hyacinthe. "I had the impression he needed glasses?"

Sister John nodded, adding generously, "but his teeth were certainly magnificent."

They experienced still another caller in the afternoon, this one a Mr. Smith from the local Cowbell Dairy, resplendent in white coveralls, who insisted on leaving a free bottle of milk with them. When he heard they would not be occupying the house long enough for regular deliveries he responded warmly by pressing another quart of milk on them, and a pint of cottage cheese.

"A very Christian man," said Sister Hyacinthe when he had gone. "People seem very neighborly here, don't they?"

"Yes, don't they?" agreed Sister John cheerfully.

They dined early on beef stew, homemade bread and cottage cheese, and were drinking comfrey tea on the back steps when Alfie emerged from the woods lugging armfuls of boards, a long saw and a duffel bag. "Hey, I'm back," he called, dumping his burden by the privet hedge. "I came as soon as I could, I had to visit the town dump to find glass for your window. Any suspicious visitors?" He looked hopeful.

"Only a census taker and a milkman," said Sister John. "It's certainly kind of you to find glass for the window."

"Actually I couldn't find glass," he said. "There weren't any old windows at the dump today so until somebody brings one in I hope you don't mind a few boards. How's Sister Ursula?"

"He's had eggnog and beef broth and Sister John is making him a nun's habit. It's already cut to size."

"By George, that's really inspired," said Alfie, looking pleased. "I wish I'd thought of that myself."

"Come in and have some tea," Sister John suggested, rising.

"I'll come in but let's wait for Naomi, she started out with me except I lost her in the woods. She stopped to pick borage," he explained, dropping into a kitchen chair. "By the way, I brought you a book." He proudly placed it on the table. "It's Brill's book. He'd never tell you about it himself, he's too modest. I thought where you've been behind walls for years you might find it interesting."

"Brill's book?"

"Yeah, he wrote it. It was published last year."

"An author?" gasped Sister Hyacinthe, impressed.

Sister John looked at the book's brilliant red jacket slashed with stripes of black. "*Underground America* by Brill Stevenson. What a strange title . . ."

"You haven't heard the phrase before? Brill used to write for the underground press. He's a social psychologist."

"In those clothes?" faltered Sister John.

"Just goes to show," Alfie said cheerfully. "Show what it's all about, I mean. The supreme irony is hiding your light under a bushel, you see. It's what the revolution is all about."

"Revolution?"

"In values," Naomi said, walking in the door with an armful of borage. She gazed around her openmouthed at the tin sink, the cupboards and the oilcloth-covered table. "Wow, this is *real* camp. Wild!"

"What does she mean?" Sister Hyacinthe asked Alfie.

"She means she likes your house, it's too corny to be true. This book," he went on, pointing a long finger at it, "brought in ten shocked reviews, six rave reviews and the New York *Times* said every American should read it as a warning. He made eight thousand bucks from it and bought two hundred acres of land in Maine, to which we will repair in September. About twenty of us. A bit of a celebrity, Brill—in some circles, anyway. You've heard of communes?" When Sister John shook her head he said, "Hippies? Yippies? Women's Lib?"

"Male chauvinist pigs?" put in Naomi. "Watergate? Kent State? Third World? Club of Rome?"

When both sisters stared at them blankly Alfie said, "Good God, you're like Martians visiting us for the first time! Is that what being in cloister means?"

"We did see that nice Mr. Glenn circle the earth," volunteered Sister John. "Mr. Armisbruck brought in a television set for us."

"But that was in 1962," he pointed out. "You'd really better read Brill's book. Oh, and he says you can both come to the meeting tonight if you'd like."

"Meeting?"

"Of the workers. They want roofs that don't leak."
He looked at them challengingly. "If you want to see
what's been happening and not happening in this world
I think you ought to go."

Sister John thought for a moment. "We must, of
course. Except—oh dear, there's Sister Ursula."

"I'll look after him," volunteered Sister Hyacinthe.

Sister John shook her head. "I couldn't possibly leave
you here alone, knowing how you feel about the
house."

"I'll stay with her," Alfie said eagerly. "I could
maybe find another secret passage. I could talk to Sister
Ursula, too, and try to find out more about him.
Nobody'll miss me at the meeting."

Sister John considered this. "We really must learn
about everything, and I do confess to an interest in what
you could be doing with farm workers." She glanced at
Sister Hyacinthe, still holding a cup of tea in one hand.
"Let's all go up to see him; it's time formal introduc-
tions were made."

It could not justly be said that Sister Ursula warmed
to Alfie and Naomi at first glance, not even after it had
been explained to him that they were neighbors and
quite harmless. His reaction upon seeing them was a vi-
olent, "Oh, God, *hippies?*"

"Already I know something about him," said Alfie.

"Definitely Establishment," said Naomi.

On the other hand, once Sister Ursula had purged
himself of this epithet he gave every evidence of relief
at seeing another male, especially since it turned out
that he had to go to the bathroom. After Alfie had carried him off down the hall they attempted a hasty fur-

nishing of his room. Lamps and a table were brought
upstairs, a bed carried down the hall to a place under
his mattress and a rug tossed across the floor. The room
began to acquire a certain lighthearted bohemian flavor,
or, in Naomi's words, it took on the look of a real pad.
All of this reduced a great deal of Sister Ursula's hostility; the remainder of it showed further signs of ero-
sion when Alfie promised him cigarettes and said he
might play a hand of poker with him after repairing the
broken window.

Naomi went back to camp alone, leaving Alfie to his
boards and hammer. Presently she returned to escort
Sister John to the meeting, carrying with her a number
of items that Alfie had requested for the evening, including cigarettes for Sister Ursula. Looking radiant,
Sister John left with a wave of her hand.

Alfie's hammering issued rhythmically from the side
of the house. Birds chattered in the tops of the trees and
a locust sang from a hidden vine of wisteria. Sister
Hyacinthe, strolling out to the porch, sat down on the
front steps and removed her shoes. The sun was an hour
to sunset, racing against a series of cumulus clouds that
threatened to blot out its brilliance before it reached the
horizon. After wriggling her toes in the grass for a few
delicious minutes Sister Hyacinthe stood up and walked
around the side of the house to look for Alfie. She
found the dining-room window neatly boarded over but
Alfie had removed himself to the rear. "The pantry window needed fixing," he explained. "Darn thing has no
lock and opened as soon as I touched it." He climbed
down and regarded his handiwork with pride. "I'd like
to see the man who could get through *that*."

"So would I," Sister Hyacinthe told him loyally.

"You notice I nailed the boards in the shape of a cross. Appropriate, don't you think, and rather artistic?"

"Oh, very."

They strolled around the opposite side of the house testing windows as they went, and entered the front door just as the clouds reached and obscured the sun, turning the world a metallic gray. This sudden withdrawal of sun dimmed the main hall and placed it in twilight. The house seemed abruptly, overwhelmingly, still, with a tomb-like quality that struck Sister Hyacinthe as extremely unpleasant. She could hear the faucet dripping in the kitchen, the rustle of ivy against the house and upstairs a snort from Sister Ursula.

Alfie said in a subdued voice, "I don't think I'll tackle the secret staircase after all."

"No," said Sister Hyacinthe.

"Of course it won't be really dark for another hour but the lights work all right, don't they?"

She nodded.

"Weird house. Very atmospheric. One feels a lot of people have died here."

"I feel it, too," said Sister Hyacinthe, "but then of course people have to die somewhere."

"Not violently. There aren't—I mean you and Sister John had no problem sleeping last night? No strange sounds or anything?"

Sister Hyacinthe gave him a sympathetic glance. "If you mean ghosts, Sister John says if you meet one you just say 'In the name of Jesus Christ go away.' "

Alfie nodded. "I wish I found that reassuring. Let's consult the I Ching about your house—I asked Naomi to bring it over. You've heard of the Book of Change? No, I don't suppose you have. I really don't think you'd find it blasphemous," he said earnestly, "unless of course you're terribly devout. Well, I suppose you are, being a nun, so you can watch. I've got the I Ching and the yarrow stalks . . . oh yes, and cigarettes and playing cards for Sister Ursula."

"That's terribly kind of you."

"I thought so."

"Is I Ching a game?" she asked, looking at the odd assortment that Alfie pulled out of his pocket.

"Good Lord, no, it's ancient Chinese divination. I wish we had some incense to burn. You don't happen to have any lying around, do you?"

Sister Hyacinthe shook her head. "Only some red cayenne pepper; it kills vermin and insects when you burn it in a closed room."

Alfie gave her an admiring glance. "I have the feeling you may appreciate the I Ching more than I expected. Let's go upstairs and begin our baby-sitting, shall we?"

They found Sister Ursula tossing restlessly on his bed. "You took so damn long," he said peevishly. "I thought at first you'd all gone off and left me and then I could hear you talking and talking down there."

"Alfie has brought you cigarettes," Sister Hyacinthe told him. "Of course they're not at all good for you—"

"Neither is being shot at," he said, looking at Alfie expectantly.

The cigarettes were produced and he immediately lighted one and sent up spirals of smoke. The curtains were drawn at the window, the lamp brought closer and the yarrow sticks unwrapped. In a solemn voice Alfie said, "We are asking about this house, we are asking if Sister Hyacinthe and Sister John will find this a happy place ..." A deep silence fell over the room as they watched Alfie toss the yarrow sticks and lay out intricate lineal arrangements on paper. Sister Ursula puffed away non-stop on his cigarettes, producing the only incense available, and Sister Hyacinthe thought it all very companionable and not unlike the abbey on a winter's evening.

Alfie said at last, "It comes out hexagram 39."

"Never heard of anything so ridiculous," said Sister Ursula, punching his pillow. "You really expect an answer?"

Alfie said coldly, "I know two more things about you: you have a New York accent and a closed mind. Okay, here's hexagram 39. Brace yourselves, it's the Chen hexagram, meaning trouble."

Sister Hyacinthe placed her hands over her ears. "I don't want to hear it."

"Well, look for yourself. It says, 'This hexagram implies great difficulties. Danger lies ahead. To perceive danger and succeed in averting it, this is wisdom indeed.' "

"I don't believe it," snorted Sister Ursula. "You're just trying to alarm me with mumbo-jumbo black magic hoping I'll tell you who shot me. Bull. I'll bet you there weren't even three men prowling around the garden last night."

"Three men in the garden?" Alfie turned to Sister Hyacinthe in astonishment. "Good God, Sister Hyacinthe, is that true?"

"Now you've done it," she told Sister Ursula reproachfully. "How did *you* know?"

"Heard you talking."

"Yes, there were three men here last night, they came

during the thunderstorm and left when Sister John called from the window."

"But that's terrible," cried Alfie. He jumped up, turned off the lights and hurried to the window to peer outside. "Good Lord, why didn't you tell me? That's just what you ought to be afraid of. If they were looking for a body in the garden they'll be trying next to get into the house."

"You're a real bundle of cheer," Sister Ursula told him. "Anybody out there?"

"No, so I'll turn on the lights again but I don't think you're so helpful, either, you know. Who wants you dead? Why were you shot?"

"No comment."

"Why?"

"Because I'm nasty clear through to the bone," he growled. "Are we going to play poker or don't hippies play poker?"

"I'm not a hippie."

"The hell you're not. I know a hippie when I see one."

Sister Hyacinthe intervened quickly. "I have to remind you both that Sister Ursula is convalescent—he's still very weak—and if you're going to play poker you'll have to play without arguing. Where are your cards, Alfie?"

From downstairs a voice called, "Hey, everybody, anybody at home?"

"It's Naomi. Up here," shouted Alfie.

"Coming," called back Naomi, her voice growing nearer. "Which room? Oh, here you are. When Brill told me Sister Hyacinthe was going to make a fresh comfrey poultice tonight I had to come and watch.

Look who just came in on the bus from New York—
I've brought Bhanjan Singh!"

Naomi appeared in the doorway wearing a long flow-
ering muslin dress, followed by a short rotund figure in
what looked to be another long and flowing dress. As
they entered the room, however, certain differences
could be noted: the second figure was male, and the
dress was a yellow robe covering a plump, twinkling
little man with beige skin and bright black eyes.

"Oh God," said Sister Ursula from his bed.

"Great," said Alfie. "Bhanjan will have ideas,
Bhanjan knows everything. He's a guru."

"Guru?" said Sister Hyacinthe blankly.

Sister Ursula, looking Bhanjan Singh over from head
to foot, said, "Christ, don't you people know any nice
Chamber of Commerce types, any TV repairmen or
stockbrokers or postmen?"

"Don't be dull," said Naomi. "Bhanjan's not only a
Tibetan monk but he can read the future if he chooses."

Sister Ursula laughed derisively. "He could start by
reading mine, then, since I don't even know if I have
one."

"Show me a man who insists on knowing the future," said Bhanjan Singh gently, "and I will show you
a man who finds the past meaningless and the present
empty. Such a man should attend to his soul, which is
undernourished."

"It can't be any more undernourished than my stomach," protested Sister Ursula. "They've given me nothing but broth and eggnog. Come on, be a sport and tell
me my future."

Bhanjan smiled and shook his head. "I will say only

this, my friend: if you cannot bear a sting you should not put your finger in a scorpion's nest."

Sister Ursula stared at him blankly.

"The Sufis also have a saying: Make no friendship with an elephant keeper if you have no room to entertain an elephant."

To Sister Hyacinthe's surprise their patient's face turned dark red, as if Bhanjan's words had scored a mysterious hit. She said, rising, "That's enough for now. Before any fresh shocks are given to Sister Ursula I'll change the poultice on his arm. I think I'll also make us a pot of sassafras tea."

"I'll help," said Naomi.

Over sassafras tea they discussed clairvoyance, and Bhanjan Singh explained that it was simply a matter of seeing the invisible: every human being carried about with him his past, his present and his future. Even a rock, he said, had an aura and characteristics all its own.

"That's hard to believe," said Sister Hyacinthe.

Bhanjan Singh looked at her with amusement. "About yourself, Sister Hyacinthe, I see that you have great compassion for green and growing things, and I believe that you have conversations with your plants and sometimes—am I not right?—you listen to them reply to you."

Alfie turned to her eagerly. "Do you really, Sister Hyacinthe? Oh, crackerjack, I knew you were one of us!"

Sister Hyacinthe had turned crimson with embarrassment. "I've never told anyone I talk to my herbs."

"You can't keep things from Bhanjan," Naomi told her. "He picks them up. He's a very advanced person."

"Maybe he is in Tibet," said Sister Ursula, "but Americans are more rational. What's your angle, Bhanjan Singh, how do you do it? Christ, you've got even me curious."

"To him who has perception," said Bhanjan, "a mere sign is enough. For him who does not really heed, a thousand explanations are not enough."

"Well, give it a try, won't you?"

Bhanjan shrugged. "It's very simple, really: all around you are clues, promises, auras, vibrations, portents. Think of electricity! We are surrounded by it but no one has ever seen it. Your physicists tell us that we have each of us a magnetic field which can be measured, and when we leave a chair in which we have been sitting we leave behind traces of this magnetic field that can be measured by instruments. In this house there remain just such traces of all the thoughts and emotions experienced here. You are accustomed only to the visible, but the most significant things in life are invisible."

"Like thought," pointed out Alfie.

"And love," added Naomi.

Sister Hyacinthe said eagerly, "How did it start, how did it come to you? Where did you begin?"

"It is something that may come only after long years of meditation," said Bhanjan. "Of stilling the mind and silencing desire."

Sister Ursula said testily, "That's all very well but you can't earn a living if you go around meditating all the time, how can you get anywhere in life?"

"Bhanjan isn't interested in getting anywhere," said Naomi. "He's already there."

"Where?"

"In a state of Being."

"Where the hell's that?" demanded Sister Ursula. "What does he do for food? Tell me how he pays his bills. For that matter how do either of you pay your bills?"

Sister Hyacinthe said seriously, "At the abbey we pay our bills by baking bread and selling it, sixty loaves a day fresh from the ovens of St. Tabitha's."

"You too?" Sister Ursula looked alarmed. "My God, am I outnumbered? Am I the only one here who pays taxes, has a job and a bank account, knows what an investment portfolio is and holds things together?"

Bhanjan Singh said gently, "You are also the only one here, my friend, with three bullet holes in him."

After Sister Ursula had fallen asleep Bhanjan Singh told them stories in the kitchen. Once upon a time, he said, when God had finished making the world, he wanted to leave behind Him for man a piece of His own divinity, a spark of His essence, a promise to man of what he could become, with effort. He looked for a place to hide this Godhead because, he explained, what man could find too easily would never be valued by him.

"Then you must hide the Godhead on the highest mountain peak on earth," said one of His councilors.

God shook His head. "No, for man is an adventuresome creature and he will soon enough learn to climb the highest mountain peaks."

"Hide it then, O Great One, in the depths of the earth!"

"I think not," said God, "for man will one day discover that he can dig into the deepest parts of the earth."

"In the middle of the ocean then, Master?"

God shook His head. "I've given man a brain, you see, and one day he'll learn to build ships and cross the mightiest oceans."

"Where then, Master?" cried His councilors.

God smiled. "I'll hide it in the most inaccessible place of all, and the one place that man will never to think look for it. I'll hide it deep inside of man himself."

Sister Hyacinthe looked at Bhanjan Singh and smiled. "Now I know what a guru is," she said simply.

6

When Sister John returned at nine o'clock they had moved into the living room and were sitting on the floor instructing Sister Hyacinthe in Buddhist meditation. She had been directed to breathe deeply through first one nostril and then the other, after which she had chanted A-u-m until her palate tickled and all of her brain cells vibrated. Following this came a stillness marred only by the hum of crickets outside, the rustle of ivy against the wall and the faraway scream of a siren somewhere along Fallen Stump Road.

Into this silence walked Sister John, looking distracted. "Sister Hyacinthe?" she called, and stopped in surprise at the sight of four bowed heads.

Alfie looked up and grinned. "Hi, Sister John, how was the meeting?"

"Heartbreaking," she said, and sank into a chair. "I don't want to talk about it until I can think about it. I've been asked by Brill to send you right back to camp because rabbits are eating the lettuce in your garden."

"There are always rabbits in the garden," sighed Naomi. "It's positively symbolic, like serpents in Eden. Hey, Sister John, you haven't met Bhanjan Singh yet."

"Singh?" echoed Sister John, and seeing him uncoil himself from the floor stared at him in astonishment; he advanced toward her and she made a move to rise.

"No, no," he said, smiling. "Please remain seated, I see that you are very tired."

"Surely we've met before?" she asked, looking baffled.

His smile deepened. "We recognize each other because we are travelers on the same path, although perhaps in another life—never mind, I want you to know that I have enjoyed this evening so much."

"They've given you tea?"

"Yes, and much more."

The sound of a siren that had remained a backdrop for their words now became loud and penetrating, like a scream gone berserk. Sister John opened her mouth and spoke but her words were swallowed up at once and soundless. Alfie walked over to the window, drew aside the curtain and peered outside. "My God, it's a police car," he gasped. "A police car coming *here*. Straight up the driveway to the house!"

"*Sister Ursula,*" cried Sister Hyacinthe, stumbling to her feet. "The police will find him!"

"No they won't, we'll hide him. Upstairs, everybody," shouted Alfie, waving his arms. "No, no, not you, Sister Hyacinthe, you live here. Come on—fast—before they reach the front door and see us."

Alfie raced for the stairs, followed by Naomi and Bhanjan Singh. "This is a frenzied world," said Sister John with a sigh and a shake of her head. "You and I must set an example of being very calm."

"Y-y-es," stammered Sister Hyacinthe, standing at the foot of the stairs and looking anything but calm.

The siren was mercifully stilled, a car door slammed, followed by heavy footsteps on the wooden stairs and a loud knock. Sister John smoothed her coif, moved to the door and opened it.

Two men in uniform confronted her, one of them middle-aged, well-muscled and formidable, the other small, elderly and wizened. "Evening, ma'am," said the larger one. "Mind if we come in?" Without waiting for reply he opened the screen door and walked past her into the hall, his glance taking in Sister Hyacinthe on the stairs before settling on Sister John. "I'm Sheriff McGee and this is Deputy Johnson."

"I'm Sister John and that's Sister Hyacinthe," she responded crisply. "May I ask what brings you at this late hour?"

"Well," he drawled in a flat bored voice, "to be perfectly frank about it, ma'am, to get to the point without horsing around, so to speak, you can pack your bags and come along with us, if you know what I mean. We've come to take you wherever you were going when you got here."

"Wherever we were going when we got here," echoed Sister John in a bewildered voice. "But as you can see, we're already here."

"Yes, ma'am, but you shouldn't *be* here, it's against the law," he said. "I don't know what rules you sisters go by, being Presbyterian myself, but you can't just stop where you please; it's trespassing."

"Trespassing?" repeated Sister John. "Is that why you've come? Is that the only reason you're here?"

"If you don't think it's reason enough I could always

add more charges," he said, eyeing her coldly. "Like breaking and entering, maybe."

"No, no, that's quite all right," she told him hastily. "Who told you we were trespassing? Who made the complaint?"

The sheriff shook his head. "I get my orders from higher up, Sister—"

"As we do, too," put in Sister John.

"—so I wouldn't know who complained, now would I? Hubie, where the hell did I put my imported SaniSmokes?" He had been absently patting his pockets; now he turned indignantly to his deputy.

"Saw you tuck 'em in your hip pocket."

"Damn fool place to put them." He brought out a large fat cigar and held it, unlighted, as he continued to explain the circumstances. "It's not a duty I take to kindly," he said, "running you off this property, but it's a private residence and trespassing's against the law, so if you'll just pack up your things and come along peaceably now—"

"Oh, we couldn't possibly," Sister John told him.

His boredom vanished in a second. "Maybe you're not reading me loud and clear," he said in a hard voice, and clamped his cigar between his teeth. "Maybe you're thinking nuns get special treatment—I've seen you people on the six o'clock news, Sister, and some of you are getting to be real troublemakers."

"We are?" said Sister John, surprised.

"Get out the handcuffs, Hubie."

"Handcuffs?" Sister John said incredulously.

"Handcuffs. Believe me, I wouldn't hesitate to carry you out, you understand me? In fact, to lay it on the line, Sister, if you're not out of here in ten minutes I'll

not only arrest you, I'll put you in jail a few days to
cool off."

Sister John stared at him in astonishment. "I never
heard such nonsense in my life, Sheriff. And you call
yourself a Presbyterian, a Christian, presumably with a
conscience?"

"You can leave my conscience out of this," he said.
"I'm tired to death of people screaming about consciences these days. Laws are *laws*. Now are you coming peaceably or do we use force?" He removed the
cigar from his mouth and returned her steady look un-
blinkingly. "Well?"

Sister John said curtly, "I'd like to get something
from the kitchen."

"Go with her, Hubie," the sheriff told his deputy.

Hubie accompanied her; a moment later Sister John
returned with a sheaf of papers bound in pale blue.
"The deed," she said, presenting it to him.

"Deed? What d'ye mean deed?"

"To this property. Which," she told him coolly, "happens to have been left quite legally to St. Tabitha's Abbey of Bridgemont, Pennsylvania, making you the
trespassers here."

"Left to you?" said the sheriff. "Christ, how can it be
left to you when it belongs to Frank Scozzafava?"

"I don't know about any Scozzafava. If you'll read
the deed you'll see it was bequeathed to us by Mr.
Moretti."

"Who the hell's Moretti?"

"The man who owned this property."

The sheriff's glance dropped to the papers in his hand
and he scowled over the first page. "Joseph A.
Moretti," he read aloud, and slowly a look of astonish-

ment replaced his scowl. "Christ, d'ye mean *Joe* Moretti?"

"Since I never had the pleasure of meeting him I've never called him that but possibly his friends did."

"Old Joe Moretti," said the sheriff incredulously. "And he left this place to *nuns*?" A rich and fruity chuckle escaped him. "Oboy," he said. "Oboy, Scozzafava's not going to like this." He began to look extremely pleased that Scozzafava wasn't going to like this. Handing the deed back to Sister John, he said, "Let's go, Hubie, it looks like we got a very very interesting night ahead of us." At the door he turned and gave Sister John a curious glance. "How many sisters you got here in this Godforsaken place?"

"Three," Sister John told him, "but there are no places that God has forsaken, Sheriff, and we have our faith."

"Hell, you may need it," he said, and disappeared into the darkness.

From the stairs came a long drawn-out sigh as Sister Hyacinthe stopped holding her breath. "You were magnificent, Sister John," she breathed. "I was terrified."

"A most extraordinary man," said Sister John, staring after him. "Pure bully—one of the most unpleasant I believe I've ever met—and what I resent very much is that I shall have to pray for him."

"Surely not yet," pleaded Sister Hyacinthe.

"He would have taken us to jail, can you imagine? And in handcuffs. I might add that he even seemed to relish the thought."

"At least we won't have to see him again," pointed out Sister Hyacinthe.

"One certainly hopes not because he strikes me as a very weak reed to lean on in crisis."

From the landing above them Alfie called down. "Why didn't they want to search the house?" He sounded offended.

"Because Sister Ursula appeared to be the last thing on the sheriff's mind. You can come down now. How's Sister Ursula?"

"Exhausted but swearing a lot. Naomi and Bhanjan are carrying him back to bed. Look, if Brill needs us we'd better leave now but first tell us what happened. What did he want?"

"There seems to have been a misunderstanding over who owns the house," Sister John told him. "After I produced the deed the sheriff transferred his considerable hostility to a man named Scozzafava, but not before he threatened to throw us out of the house. Would you believe he was going to send Sister Hyacinthe and me to jail, and very happily, too?"

"I could believe it," Alfie said, nodding. "God, I hate leaving. To think we have to exchange all this for chasing rabbits."

"Must we?" protested Naomi, following Bhanjan Singh down the stairs.

"Try to remember," pointed out Bhanjan Singh, "that every plain is followed by a slope, every going forth is followed by a return." He paused to shake hands with Sister Hyacinthe, his eyes twinkling. "Next time chamomile?" At the door he stopped and directed a penetrating glance at Sister John. "A word of warning," he said softly. "There is evil all around you here. To tread with impunity upon a tiger's tail, breathless caution is required." Shepherding Alfie and Naomi in front of him, he went out.

"I don't like the sound of that," said Sister Hyacinthe, staring after him. "Bhanjan Singh knows things."

"Yes, what a dear little man he is, and what an astonishing day this has been," said Sister John. "Except— where has it gone? I want to begin reading Brill's book, I want to think about the migrant workers I met tonight, there's Sister Ursula's habit to finish, I want to hear about Bhanjan Singh, and I simply *must* write Mother Angelique and ask about Sister Emma." She turned off the hall lights and moved to the door to close and lock it for the night. "Sister Hyacinthe, look—the moon is out now!"

Sister Hyacinthe came to stand beside her and they gazed out on a brilliant, cloudless sky. A huge globe of a moon hung over the thruway, dusting their lawn with silver and sending inky long fingers across the hollows. With a catch in her voice Sister Hyacinthe said, "It's *such* a beautiful world, isn't it, Sister John?"

Off to their left a shadow detached itself from the shrubbery and the dark figure of a man moved through the tall grass toward the center of the lawn. For a moment he stood quietly in the moonlight, his face hidden from them, and then he turned and stared up at the house and with his head lifted they clearly saw his features: it was the garbage man, Mr. Quigley. They had no sooner recognized him than he glided across the lawn—there was no other way to describe his well-oiled soundless movement—and vanished around the side of the house.

"Really," said Sister John thoughtfully, "when you

recall that this property has been deserted for years it seems an amazingly busy place."

Sister Hyacinthe only shivered. "Close the door, Sister John, I don't like it, it frightens me."

After evening prayers they carefully locked up the house and carried a glass of warm milk to Sister Ursula. They spread their bedrolls across mattresses in the room next to their patient, but Sister John said she refused to go to bed until she had read some of Brill's book, whereupon she went downstairs and established herself under a lamp in the living room.

Sister Hyacinthe washed her face, brushed her teeth and knelt beside her bed. After a few minutes on her knees, and hearing only snores from Sister Ursula's room, she dropped to the floor, crossed her legs under her and tried a tentative Ahhhhh and then an Ooooooo, followed by an Mmmmmmmm.

In the living room Sister John opened *Underground America* to its Preface and began to read. *Once upon a time*, she read, *there was a United States of America where Sunday dinner was roast beef and apple pie, where the Fourth of July was parades, the American flag, and a lump in the throat; where any little boy could grow up to be President and every little girl waited patiently to trade her Barbie doll for a real baby after she met Prince Charming, with whom she would live happily forever after. . . .*

Today roast beef is $3. a pound and the apple pie full of chemicals; there have been a few problems about the American flag which has been flown upside down, backwards and at half mast too many times; Vietnam and Watergate have removed the last vestiges of America's *fabled innocence; the divorce rate is zooming, the air polluted, our water dirty . . .*

Oblivious to the sounds of humming from Sister Hyacinthe's room upstairs, and of snoring from Sister Ursula's room, Sister John moved from Preface to Chapter One, her eyes growing wider and wider.

7

In the morning Sister Hyacinthe opened her eyes to a chorus of bird song and lay in bed recalling the events of the previous evening. Sister John, she noticed, had already awakened and gone downstairs, leaving her bedroll neatly folded at the foot of her bed. Sister Hyacinthe wondered if she had left her magnetic field behind her, too. The thought of that rotund little man Bhanjan Singh filled her with the greatest pleasure. She could not have put it into words but she felt that most of the obstacles in her life had been placed there by logical people. Bhanjan Singh, on the other hand, was a man who had mastered logic and then happily left it behind him for a world that Sister Hyacinthe sometimes glimpsed but had never dared mention to others, fearing ridicule.

Rising, she said her prayers, dressed and went downstairs to look for Sister John. She could find traces of her everywhere: Brill's book open on the couch, Sister Ursula's habit neatly folded on the kitchen table, their breakfast gruel simmering on the stove. She called and a moment later Sister John emerged from the cellar wreathed in cobwebs. "I've been in the preserve closet," she said breathlessly.

"*That* disagreeable place!"

"I've just hidden the money there. I had trouble sleeping last night," she confessed. "I came downstairs and finished Sister Ursula's habit, and then I wrote a long letter to our abbess asking her about Sister Emma and telling her about the suitcase. Then it occurred to me that of course she'll want to know how much money is *in* the suitcase so I carried it down to the preserve closet where we can count it later, whenever we have time. Which brings me," she added, "to the suitcase."

"Suitcase," echoed Sister Hyacinthe.

She nodded. "I know Sister Vincent would love to have it for her lute but last night I met someone with more pressing needs. A little girl named Alice, Sister Hyacinthe."

Sister Hyacinthe stopped spooning out the gruel and waited, spoon in hand.

"I can talk about it now but it upset me a great deal," confessed Sister John, her voice trembling a little. "You can't imagine how those migrant workers live, Sister Hyacinthe. This child, this little girl, is nine years old and hasn't the faintest concept of what a home is. She and her family move week after week, wherever crops need to be picked, and she carries her few things with her in a paper bag." There were tears in Sister John's eyes; she reached into her sleeve for a handkerchief. "Her dream, Sister Hyacinthe, is to own a little suitcase. She saw one once in a picture. Before that she'd never known suitcases existed for the"—Sister John's lip curled—"for the *traveler*." Anger drove the tears from her eyes and she returned the handkerchief to her sleeve.

"And the child's American?" asked Sister Hyacinthe in astonishment.

"Of course she's American, although if you asked her she might not know what that means. She's an outcast, Sister Hyacinthe, every single one of those migrant workers is an outcast."

"But why?" asked Sister Hyacinthe, bewildered.

"It's all in Brill's book," Sister John said firmly. "Apathy. Nobody knows who's in charge any more. The center no longer holds."

"But people who believe in God, surely—"

Sister John shook her head. "According to Brill's book *Time* magazine announced in 1966 that God is dead. Terrible things have been happening in the world, Sister Hyacinthe. It's hard to understand, and it would look utterly hopeless to me if I hadn't seen for myself, with my own eyes—" She hesitated.

"Seen what?" asked Sister Hyacinthe, and put down her cup of clover blossom tea.

"Seen what these young people are doing. Brill insists it's nothing, he says it's nothing because they'll soon be abandoning the workers just like everybody else but that isn't so, because without any thought of recompense—only because they want to, because they care—they've been spending their free time with them, explaining their rights to them. Simple things, like how to get a birth certificate—can you believe that most of them don't have one?—and how to insist on enough money and enough plumbing, and how to fight horrid crew leaders. It's a beautiful thing, Sister Hyacinthe."

"What are crew leaders?"

"Men who hire the workers down south and bring them up here in trucks or cars and pay them. And steal from them, too, frequently."

"Sister *John!*"

"Exactly. They are absolutely helpless people, Sister Hyacinthe." Her chin tilted defiantly. "It may be shocking of me to say but I find it hard to believe that hell is off somewhere in another world after learning how these people live on this earth."

"I'm not shocked," Sister Hyacinthe said loyally. "What are you going to do?" She asked this as a matter of course, knowing that it was Sister John's nature to fix and change things.

"I don't know yet," Sister John said, idly stirring her tea. "Brill is going to come over this afternoon and tell me more about them. Perhaps I could begin by writing an article for our magazine. After all, *Reflections* has a judge and three doctors on its mailing list."

"I've often wondered if anyone actually *reads* our magazine," Sister Hyacinthe said boldly.

Sister John gave her a level, expressionless glance.

"Or whether they're just loyal Catholics," finished Sister Hyacinthe, and stood up and carried her empty bowl to the sink.

"You may have a point," said Sister John with a wry smile, "but it's one I hope you'll never repeat to Sister Charity, it would break her heart. I wonder if you'd mind taking up Sister Ursula's breakfast tray while I spread out the money for counting downstairs. Has he had meat yet?"

"He had it in his stew last night."

Sister John nodded. "Then give him gruel this morning." She left the table and walked into the pantry. "All these jars of sugar will have to be moved out of here and down to the preserve closet, Sister Hyacinthe, they take up far too much space. I see you didn't even have room to put away all the groceries yesterday." Her skirts rustled; Sister John's habit was always more crisply starched than anybody else's.

"Sugar?"

"Yes, jars of it everywhere."

Sister Hyacinthe winced. "And I bought sugar yesterday. Five pounds of it."

"I thought you might have noticed. Come see for yourself."

Sister Hyacinthe joined her in the pantry and discovered that two long high shelves were crammed with large glass jars labeled powdered sugar. At a glance it looked as if their pantry was stocked with more than fifty pounds of the stuff, and her apologies for buying more of it were fervent.

"No harm done. Mr. Moretti was, I fear, a hoarder. Obviously a hoarder." Picking up three of the jars, Sister John added, "You might bring a few down later." Clutching the jars to her bosom, she moved at a slant toward the cellar door, kicked it wide with the toe of one boot and disappeared.

Sister Ursula did not appreciate the gruel. After one mouthful his eyes bulged, he swallowed with difficulty, and gagged. "What the hell is this stuff?" he gasped.

"Gruel," said Sister Hyacinthe. "It's no more gluey than oatmeal and just as nutritious."

"Yes but what *is* it?"

"Slippery elm bark, cooked and flavored with nutmeg and honey."

"God damn," he exploded. "I'm used to bacon and eggs every morning, lots of toast and jam, fruit juice and coffee and you're feeding me tree bark?"

"Cooked tree bark."

"Horrible," he said, shuddering. "The kindest thing I can say for it is that it must have a hell of a low cholesterol count."

Sister Hyacinthe nodded. "Attitude is so important, don't you think? Try another spoonful before it gets cold, it tends to jell when it's cold. You might as well like it because you'll be having it for breakfast tomorrow, too."

"The death of hope," he growled. "What are you planning for lunch, shrubbery and grubs?"

"Bread, cheese and tea," she said, grinning at him. "I think you're developing a sense of humor, Sister Ursula, you must be feeling better."

"A person would have to develop something here. Ulcers, hives, eczema," he said gloomily. "The thing is, I'm not used to the ascetic sort of life."

"I didn't think you were," she said. "What kind are you accustomed to?"

"Comfort and money. In case you've never noticed, comfort is what money buys, the more money the more comfort, and I wish you wouldn't look as if you don't know what I'm talking about. I'm talking about things like two-hundred-dollar suits and—oh no, you don't," he said, eyes narrowing. "Tricked me, didn't you. We were talking about today's menu and I was going to ask you what's for dinner—if I dare."

"Probably beef stew again," she said frankly, "but if Alfie brings us eggs there'll be mushroom omelet. Sister John says you're to stand up and try taking a few steps today."

"It'll give me an appetite," he warned her. "You understand I'm in no hurry to leave but I'll feel a lot safer when I can walk. Or run," he added cryptically. "Is Sister John planning to convert me?"

"She's started praying hard for your soul."

He nodded. "She has a very firm chin, I was afraid of that."

"Well, you have to pay a price for everything," Sister Hyacinthe told him, removing his tray, and decided that it might be kind to warn him of certain other events lying in wait for him. "Sister John has made you a kind of—well, a sort of costume, so that you'll look like a Sister Ursula."

His eyes narrowed; he said suspiciously, "Nobody's getting my pants away from me, Sister."

"But I'm sure the skirt can go right over your pants," she told him consolingly. "The coif may slip a bit, we didn't have the right kind of cloth, but the veil will almost cover it, and—"

She was drowned out by the uproar, and sensibly fled the string of profanities, bitter epithets and protests that poured from him like blood out of a pierced artery, but they followed her all the way down the stairs. She continued down another level, groping her way through the twilight of the cellar toward the preserve closet, where she reported the conversation to Sister John.

Sister John had dumped the contents of the suitcase into bushel baskets and was sorting the bills into tidy piles according to their denominations. "I can't imagine how he became that rich with such an unpleasant disposition," she said.

"It means he's getting better," Sister Hyacinthe told her. "Sick people always get cross as they get better. I rather like him, you know, I've always understood unpleasant people better than happy people."

Sister John gave her a quick glance. "I'll go up and talk to him soon. Certainly if he's getting better it doesn't leave us a great deal of time. Have you noticed how enormous the pile of one-hundred bills is growing? I'm not finding many twenties at all."

"What did you mean about time?" asked Sister Hyacinthe.

"Time to help him," pointed out Sister John. "Once he can walk I think he should join us in prayers." Her glance lifted to the blank wall and she regarded its bricks with a delicate frown. "I'm not at all sure how it can be done, Sister Hyacinthe, but I'm determined that when Sister Ursula leaves us no one will want to shoot him again. He'll be a changed man, radiating goodness."

"I think," said Sister Hyacinthe in an alarmed voice, "I'll do some pruning now."

An hour and a half later Sister John emerged from the cellar looking dazed, hurried through the house calling Sister Hyacinthe, and found her on the ladder at the corner of the house. "Sister Hyacinthe, you won't believe it," she gasped. "You simply won't believe it but I've just reached—and not even half the money counted!"

Sister Hyacinthe looked down at her warily. "Don't upset the ladder, Sister John. Reached what?"

"I've been counting the money and I've just reached ninety-nine thousand dollars."

Sister Hyacinthe stared down at her in astonishment. "But that's a great deal of money."

"Of course it is, and not half the bills counted yet. I *could* reach one hundred thousand before lunch."

"If you don't get blood poisoning first from spider bites," said Sister Hyacinthe, and climbed down the ladder to pluck an especially large black spider from Sister John's coif. "It scares me," she said.

"The spider?"

"The money. There's something wrong about it, I know there is. No house should have a man in a closet and ninety-nine thousand dollars down a well. It's just as Bhanjan Singh said, there's evil here, Sister John."

"Of course there is, but we're here now," pointed out Sister John. "You mustn't let your imagination run away with you, Sister Hyacinthe. Evil is, after all, only a deficiency of goodness."

"You mean like a vitamin deficiency?" said Sister Hyacinthe doubtfully. "I'm sorry but all I feel is nervous, Sister John. There's Sister Ursula upstairs, and ninety-nine thousand dollars downstairs, and men poking around the garden—What's that?" she asked anxiously.

A sudden roar from the trees along the road caused her to turn in time to see a motorcycle hurtle through the ivy along Fallen Stump Road and head up the driveway toward the house. It was difficult to decipher just who might be under the striped helmet and behind the enormous goggles but the display of white teeth was friendly. The motorcycle came to a halt beside them and when the goggles were shoved back and the Martian helmet removed it was Naomi. "Hi, it's my day off today, need anything from town?" she asked.

"You're the answer to a prayer, you can mail a letter for us," Sister John told her. Approaching the motorcycle she reached out and wistfully touched the chrome handlebars, tenderly following their curve down to the shining rear-view mirror. "What a glorious machine. Is it yours?"

"Like it? It's a secondhand trail bike. Eighty-nine cc four-stroke engine with overhead cam."

"Extraordinary," said Sister John, bending over to study the engine. "Sister Hyacinthe, wouldn't this be a wonderful idea for us at St. Tabitha's?"

"No," said Sister Hyacinthe. "Will Bhanjan Singh be over today?"

"Not until the weekend. He went back to New York on the bus last night and Sunrise went with him to visit friends. But," said Naomi, seeing Sister Hyacinthe's disappointment, "Alfie's bringing over eggs during his lunch hour. Where's the letter you want mailed? Why don't you come along with me?" she asked Sister John. "You can sit behind, hold on tight, and mail the letter yourself. We'll be back in an hour."

Sister Hyacinthe said in a shocked voice, "You mustn't, Sister John."

"Of course I mustn't," said Sister John, "but I don't see what harm it would do."

"Your legs will show."

"Inevitably, but there are all those new nuns with legs and I have a pair, too." She gazed measuringly at the cycle and nodded. "Yes, I believe I'd like to go. I won't be long, at least I don't think so. Where are we going, Naomi?"

"'Post office, bank, five-and-dime store, and hardware store."

"After which I'll be back," promised Sister John. "Go for a walk in the woods, count the you-know-what, or have lunch." Holding up her skirts she climbed on and sat smiling radiantly at Sister Hyacinthe until Naomi kicked the starter. The engine roared and the cycle jumped; Sister John's right hand seized Naomi's waist, her left hand flew to her veil and they zoomed off down the driveway with Sister John's skirts billowing up behind her like a balloon.

Feeling somewhat abandoned and trying not to remember she was alone except for the dubious support of Sister Ursula, Sister Hyacinthe wandered over to the steps and sat down. A ladybug was making slow progress along the step and she removed a twig of wisteria from its path. This done, she observed the fields of mustard and entertained the thought of harvesting and drying it the next day. This cheered her and she began to think how she might put together a few drying frames; she had seen some battered window screens somewhere that would serve her purpose nicely if she could only remember where she had seen them. She rose and crossed the porch to the front door, opened it and stopped in the doorway as she heard new sounds from the driveway. Through the wisteria she saw a long gray car moving toward the house, the sun glancing off its windshield and nearly blinding her. It was a very large car, she noticed as it neared the house, and it purred with a well-bred elegance that was a number of decibels below the sound of Naomi's motorcycle.

The car stopped. A square short man climbed out, picked up a briefcase and walked up the steps until, seeing Sister Hyacinthe in the shadows, he paused and gave her a twinkling smile of surprise. "Beautiful afternoon. Am I perhaps addressing the mother superior?" he asked.

"No, of course not," said Sister Hyacinthe indignantly.

"John M. Ianicelli here, purveyor of fine religious objets d'art. Crosses, rosaries, crucifixes of gold and silver, ivory, plastic and alabaster. May I come in?"

Sister Hyacinthe opened her mouth to say no; she was in fact certain that she did say no and later could not explain exactly how he succeeded in opening the door and inserting himself past her. It was masterfully done; he didn't even cause her skirts to flutter.

"*What* a charming house," he said, standing in the hall and looking up and down the stairs and into the living room. "Wonderful proportions. Starting a convent here?"

"No," said Sister Hyacinthe. "We don't need any crosses and rosaries, either."

"Wait until you see them," he confided. "Every one of them a work of art. Inexpensive, too. Where's a table?" Deaf to Sister Hyacinthe's protests he moved into the living room and placed his briefcase on the mahogany lamp table. With one hand on the lock he glanced at her. "Like to call the other sisters?"

"They're s-s-sleeping," Sister Hyacinthe stammered, and desperately wished that Sister John were here to deal with this persistent man. "And we *truly* don't need any crosses. I told you."

"Of course you told me," he said reassuringly. "I heard you, too, but I'd be a poor salesman, now wouldn't I, if I didn't show you what I've got to offer? We're both selling religion, is how I look at it. You wouldn't give up on a poor soul who says he's not interested in God, would you?"

Sister Hyacinthe felt instinctively that his reasoning was faulty; she could not quite see the analogy but felt helpless in the face of his ruthless charm. Nor did he give her time to think; with a dramatic flourish he unlocked the briefcase and opened it wide like a magician producing a white rabbit. A beam of sunlight peeping through the newly pruned windows sent a ray of light across the contents of the case and struck fire on row after row of gold and silver objects nesting on black velvet. Seeing her face he said triumphantly, "Beautiful, didn't I tell you?"

In spite of herself Sister Hyacinthe moved nearer, drawn by the glitter after years of frugality. She had never in her life seen such brilliance, and involuntarily one hand went out to touch a cross thickly encrusted with green, red and white jewels. The colors blazed like lights under water.

"Five dollars," said Mr. Ianicelli.

Sister Hyacinthe's hand withdrew quickly.

"Of course we give a large discount to nuns," said Mr. Ianicelli, "and an even bigger one on quantity purchases. Go ahead and try it on, I don't mind."

Sister Hyacinthe picked it up and found the stones thick and prickly as barnacles and warm to the touch.

"Take your time, look 'em all over," said Mr. Ianicelli. "You don't mind if I get a glass of water from your kitchen, do you? It's the hottest day we've had this summer and I'm as dry as a snake's belly."

Sister Hyacinthe was only vaguely aware that he disappeared; she held the cross up to the light and smiled as the sun struck rainbowed prisms across it. She was returned to the moment only when she heard the back door slam and Alfie shout, "Hey, what the hell do you think you're doing here?"

Conscience-stricken, Sister Hyacinthe dropped the cross back into the case and turned as Alfie herded an indignant Mr. Ianicelli back into the living room. "Sister Hyacinthe, this man was in your pantry!"

"Pantry," Sister Hyacinthe repeated blankly. "I think he said he was going to get a glass of water."

"Which is just what I was doing," said Mr. Ianicelli, his voice aggrieved, "except it's been years since I've seen an old-fashioned pantry and I stopped to look at it. Sister, who *is* this young man?"

"Never mind who I am," Alfie told him. "Who the hell are you, begging Sister Hyacinthe's pardon? Except whoever you are I jolly well think you'd better apologize and get out."

"I sell crucifixes, crosses and religious objets d'art," said Mr. Ianicelli with dignity, "and I am not accustomed to being attacked by wild-eyed hoodlums."

"That's all very well but how did you happen to know there were nuns here to show your stuff to?"

Sister Hyacinthe had not considered this fact before, and looked questioningly at Mr. Ianicelli. Without replying he walked stiffly to his suitcase, snapped it shut, then saw Sister Hyacinthe watching him and opened it again. "Here," he said, drawing out a large, ornate silver cross. "Take this for yourself, Sister, compliments of J. M. Ianicelli. A little souvenir to a sweet and gracious lady, even if your friends are insultingly rude." With a cold glance at Alfie he carried the silver cross to the mantel and placed it there, picked up his case and strode out of the living room, through the hall and down the steps. A moment later the car door slammed and they heard the purr of its engine.

"How long had he been here?" demanded Alfie.

"About ten minutes," she said, tears flooding her eyes. "If you hadn't come—He just walked *in*, Alfie, and he just kept talking, and I couldn't think what to do, with Sister John gone, and then when he showed the crosses they were so beautiful."

"Sleight of hand," said Alfie knowingly. "He didn't try to go upstairs?"

She shook her head and a tear made its way down one cheek.

"But I found him at the door to the pantry," he said, frowning. "Standing there and looking around, and I must say it shocked the daylights out of me. I didn't like his vibes. I wish you wouldn't cry, Sister Hyacinthe. Do you think I was unreasonably rude?"

"He did leave me a cross," pointed out Sister Hyacinthe, blowing her nose. "Of course it's not the cross I was admiring but it *was* very kind of him." She walked over to the mantel and picked it up, turning it over in her palm and studying it. "It's a rather vulgar cross, I wish he'd left me the other one."

"Anyway I didn't drop the eggs when I saw him," said Alfie. "I brought half a dozen and left them on the kitchen table. You'd better put them away."

He led her into the kitchen to show her six brown eggs resting precariously in the center of the table, and Sister Hyacinthe revived. "Aren't they beautiful! I've never understood how anyone can doubt God after seeing an egg. Would you like some lunch, Alfie?"

Alfie conceded that he would love some lunch, and they were munching contentedly on bread and sage cheese when Sister John returned. Her trip into town had left her dazzled by the possibility of new worlds. She had not only mailed her letter to St. Tabitha's by special delivery but at Naomi's suggestion—an inspired suggestion, she said—she had placed a long-distance telephone call to Mr. Armisbruck. It had taken time to reach him but he had promised to make a special trip to the abbey before dinner and tell the abbess how terribly important it was that they know more about Sister Emma.

"About Sister Emma!" exclaimed Sister Hyacinthe, disappointed. "Is that all?"

"It's what I particularly want to know," Sister John told her firmly. "It was delightful talking to him, Sister Hyacinthe, he said it's raining in Pennsylvania today—a very light rain—and he's charging sixty-two cents now for abbey bread."

"Highway robbery. *We* had a man selling crosses and rosaries at the house."

But Sister John gave no evidence of sharing Alfie's indignation over Mr. Ianicelli after hearing the story. Brill was coming over shortly to answer all her questions about the migrant workers and her mind was clearly occupied by this forthcoming treat. Finding communication at a standstill, Sister Hyacinthe announced that she would go into the woods to look for food, and Alfie, after a glance at his watch, said that he would go with her.

"I must say she's pretty cool about that Ianicelli guy," he complained as they crossed the lawn and entered the woods. "I thought she'd ask right away how he knew there were nuns living here. After all, you've been here only two days, haven't you?"

"She'll get to it," Sister Hyacinthe told him. "She likes crossword puzzles and she has perfect faith, you know, besides managing everything so well. She'll probably become an abbess one day although I just hope," she added darkly, "that she won't have us all on motorcycles."

"I wish you'd explain why you want to be cloistered," Alfie asked. "Don't you *mind*?"

"Mind? Of course not, it brings us nearer to God," Sister Hyacinthe said, surprised. "If you're interrupted all the time how can you possibly concentrate? Our prayers go straight up to God."

"How can you be sure?"

"We just know," she told him simply. "Shall we take this new path? I see jack-in-the-pulpits up ahead."

They wandered deeper into the woods, Sister Hyacinthe adding various leaves and roots to her basket: scallions, borage, primrose and mints. Veering off to the right to avoid a marshy bog they came out on a clearing occupied, to Sister Hyacinthe's surprise, by a long aluminum house trailer. It fairly bristled with antennas and wires that ran toward a post; one antenna resembled a glittering steel spider's web, the other, a clothesline. "My goodness," she said. "Who lives here?"

"Oh, that's Quigley's place," Alfie said in an offhand voice. "We must have taken a wrong turning."

"I've never seen such a beautiful trailer, can we look inside?"

"I wouldn't," he said with a shake of his head.

"Is his wife there?"

"Quigley married?" The idea seemed to amuse Alfie.

"I can't picture it, although one never knows, of course."

Sister Hyacinthe stared at the trailer, puzzled by something in Alfie's voice and by the look of the trailer simply dropped into the tall grass. "You're right," she said, nodding. "A woman would have planted a garden or seen to it that the grass was cut. He lives there alone then?"

"Well, he has a lot of short-wave radios and that sort of thing."

"And just collects garbage?"

"Just collects garbage," Alfie said solemnly. "Shall we find the other path now? He must hate to be spied on."

They retreated, stumbling into a glade carpeted by wild strawberries and so bright with sunshine that each of them promptly sat down without another word and began picking and eating them.

"This is great," said Alfie after an interval, rolling over in the moss. "I've forgotten it's my lunch hour, I've even forgotten Mr. Ianicelli, Sister Hyacinthe. All this sun, and I haven't tasted anything so ambrosial in weeks as these berries. Who's Mr. Ianicelli anyway? A nice guy trying to sell crosses. A nice, even thoughtful, salesman."

"Not really so thoughtful," Sister Hyacinthe pointed out unforgivingly. "He said the cross I admired cost five dollars. The cross he gave me cost five dollars, too, and if he'd been really thoughtful he would have given me the one I liked."

Alfie grinned. "I didn't realize nuns could be so human. How do you *know* the two crosses are the same price?"

"Because of the price tag," said Sister Hyacinthe patiently. "I picked up the cross he left on the mantel and there was a tiny sticker on the back that said five dollars, which is exactly what he said was the price of the jeweled cross."

Alfie gave her a long thoughtful look. "That's sort of funny, you know? I mean, if I were slightly paranoid . . ." He stopped and considered this. "A salesman who leaves for a drink of water the minute he gets a customer hooked on his merchandise . . . then leaves you with a particular cross but not the one you admired . . . I mean, if he *did* come to the house to look around—if he was looking for Sister Ursula, for instance, and if I were really suspicious . . ." He closed his mouth with a snap. "I am," he said. "Sister Hyacinthe, let's get back to the house on the double. Never mind your shoes—*run!*"

8

Sister John had carried glasses of peppermint tea to the living room where she and Brill sat on the couch, maps and papers between them. "That's how it works," he said, his finger tracing lines on the map. "It begins in Florida in early spring when they follow the sun and the crops up north. It's beans, tomatoes, berries, fruits and then back to Florida in November for the oranges, and then it's early spring and they start all over again."

Sister John said, puzzled, "I don't understand. When and where do the children go to school?"

"Often they don't," Brill said. "Two weeks in one town, one week in another—they soon get discouraged. They don't learn much, they only learn how different they are from the other kids. It's humiliating for them. That's how the system perpetuates itself because the only thing that will change them is education, and to get schooling they'd have to stay in one place. It's practically a conspiracy against them. By ten or eleven the kids are burnt out, old. They're often married by fourteen and parents at fifteen. No way out."

"There has to be a way out," said Sister John.

"Try and find it," he told her angrily. "The incredible thing is their stoicism. I don't mean they accept their life, they know damn well they deserve more. You get the feeling there's nothing for them except endurance. When they can't endure any longer they just give up and die. It's one more case of the human spirit being degraded over and over again. They just go on and on, beans today, peas tomorrow, sometimes a day off, more often not, the same backaches, same fields, same highways over and over and over."

"A nightmare," agreed Sister John and added sadly, "I don't suppose they believe in God?"

"Surprisingly they do," said Brill. "Lord knows there's nobody else they can turn to for a reward. I get no sense of grief from them when someone is killed in one of those lousy trucks or dies of malnutrition. When I first met them I thought they were damn insensitive, but now I realize they're actually glad when someone dies, there's a kind of awe that God has released them. From the wheel, you might say."

"The wheel," repeated Sister John quietly. "How terrible, when this is America where they live. Is there no joy at all in their lives, then, no kind of *earthly* release, however small? Surely a moving picture or a little shopping trip into town—"

"Oh but they never go into town," Brill said flatly.

She looked at him in surprise. "Why?"

"It's part of the conspiracy, that's all," he said, shrugging contemptuously. "They even travel at night, when people in the towns are sleeping, it's how they're kept invisible. They're warned against ever going into a town. I might add that their fears of the town are not exaggerated," Brill said dryly. "They get arrested rather quickly because of their clothes, their innocence, and *there's nobody to get them out of jail.* You have your order behind you to back you up, I have parents, a certain confidence born of affluence and a whole web of relationships. They have no one to speak for them, so of course it's safer for them to huddle together for protection and avoid towns."

"I've never heard of such a thing," Sister John said indignantly. "Now *that's* something that can be changed, it's something even I can change. Of course they must go into town, I'll take them myself."

"Now look, Sister John, there's a reason behind everything and you can't just—" He broke off as the back door slammed, footsteps raced through the house and Alfie ran into the living room. He stopped at sight of them and with exaggerated politeness said, "Hello there."

Sister Hyacinthe followed, looking distraught and saying, "But what did you *mean*, Alfie?"

"Nothing at all, go right on talking," Alfie said, and nonchalantly strolled toward the mantel. He picked up the silver cross, looked at it, carried it over to the window and held it up to the light.

"Alfie, what's wrong?" protested Sister Hyacinthe.

Alfie paid no attention. He was studying the piece of jewelry, which was complicated and baroque, a piece of flat silver to which a three-dimensional silver rose had been grafted. The stem of the rose ran vertically up to the intersection of the cross, where it blossomed out into an intricate flower with sharp petals and a bud. It

was this protuberance that he examined with narrowed
eyes.

"What *is* it?" asked Sister Hyacinthe, while Sister
John and Brill watched in astonishment from the couch.

Alfie brought a penknife from his pocket, selected
the thinnest point out of several possibilities and inserted it into the heart of the rose.

"Alfie—my cross!" cried Sister Hyacinthe, and then
stared openmouthed as the silver rose was severed from
its background and a tiny black cylinder fell into the
palm of Alfie's hand.

He dropped it to the floor and placed a foot on it,
squashing it. "*That's* why he gave you this particular
cross," he said triumphantly. "It's bugged."

The word catapulted Brill from the sofa. "You've got
to be kidding," he said, and dropped to his knees,
picked up the broken pieces and stared at them. "By
God it looks like it. Douse it in water, Alfie, it may still
be working."

"But what kind of bug?" asked Sister John, following
him into the kitchen. "In this climate there aren't any
dangerous insects, I'm sure of it."

"This," said Alfie, dropping it into a pan of water, "is
an electronic bug for eavesdropping. *Somebody* went to
a great deal of trouble to find out what you and Sister
Hyacinthe talk about in this house."

"Talk about?" Sister John looked at him as if he had
gone mad. "How on earth can you think that? How do
you even know about such things?"

"Our generation is quite advanced, we watched the
Watergate hearings."

"Watergate," repeated Sister John. "That's chapter

nineteen but I've only reached chapter fourteen in Brill's book." She stared at the glittering little black pebble underwater. "It's so tiny, how can it *be* anything?"

"Everything's transistorized these days," said Brill, picking it up. "It's actually a tiny microphone that carries the sound of your voices out to—"

"Yeah, out to where?" asked Alfie.

"Probably to a parked car," Brill said. "No, Alfie, don't go looking, the more important thing is to puzzle out what was picked up by the bug before you had your brain wave."

"No, there's something even more important than that," Alfie said abruptly. "The pantry. Ianicelli was standing by the pantry when I first saw him."

"Doing what?"

Alfie narrowed his eyes, remembering. "He was standing there staring into the pantry and looking pleased."

"Pleased?"

"Like a cat that's just swallowed a canary. A purring expression on his face. Do you think he could have bugged the pantry too?"

They hurried from sink to pantry and began a tedious search of all the shelves but they found no further signs of bugging. "I don't think he had the time anyway," insisted Sister Hyacinthe. "He left the living room and about three minutes later I heard Alfie come in and shout at him."

"Well, there doesn't seem to be any bug here," said Brill, "but you'd better hurry up and disguise Sister Ursula because, damn it, somebody's determined to—to—"

"Yes, what?" asked Sister Hyacinthe.

"Get themselves into this house, or you out of it," said Alfie.

Sister John, closing the door of the pantry, conceded this to be a possible conclusion. "In which case the most logical move would be to call in the police, except that any move to call in Sheriff McGee would not be logical, and in any case Sister Ursula is probably wanted by the police. Or so we must assume until he decides to talk."

"What do you suggest then?" asked Sister Hyacinthe.

Sister John's smile was unexpected and dazzling. "That we all keep an open mind and wait for more clues, which I believe is one of the requisites of detective work."

"I don't want to be a detective," Sister Hyacinthe said gloomily. "I came here to help you take inventory."

"Inventory seems to include Mr. Ianicelli as well as Sister Ursula," pointed out Sister John, "and now that I think about it I have a few doubts about Mr. Giovianni, too."

"Who the devil's Mr. Giovianni?" asked Brill.

"He was taking the town census yesterday and wanted to know how many people are occupying the house."

"And you believed him?" gasped Alfie.

"Of course I believed him," Sister John said impatiently. "He had a clipboard."

"Yes, and Mr. Ianicelli had rosaries."

"Of course I understand *now* that things are no longer what they appear to be, but Mr. Armisbruck, although a Lutheran, is always what he appears to be, and he's been the extent of our experience until Monday."

Sister Hyacinthe's eyes were on Alfie, who was staring transfixed at the table and smiling. "What is it, Alfie?"

He looked up with eyes shining. "I've just gotten this perfectly wonderful idea. Look at the pattern: Sister Ursula is shot and left for dead. . . . The next night three men come back, presumably looking for his remains—think how they felt when they couldn't find any!—so they send Mr. Ianicelli with a bug to find out if Sister Ursula's *inside* the house. If my theory's correct then what they're really looking for is reassurance that Sister Ursula's dead."

"But he isn't," pointed out Sister Hyacinthe.

"No, but if we could persuade Sister Ursula to give us his name—just his name, mind you—I could impersonate him. I could sign into a motel using his name—that would draw attention from this house wouldn't it?—or you could smear me with blood and I could stagger into a doctor's office saying I've been shot."

Brill grinned. "You're slipping, Alfie. What happens when it becomes obvious the motel room is empty, or when the doctor says, Okay, let's have a look at those bullet holes?"

"All right, so maybe it's a bit creaky but the point is sound. There has to be *some* way to get these people off Sister John's back."

"There is," Brill said. "Get the guy into the nun's habit in a hurry, pray hard and let Mr. Ianicelli puzzle out what happened to Sister Ursula. In the mean-

time"—he glanced at his watch—"this is—or was—our
lunch hour and we've got to get back to bean picking.
Sister John, we'll talk some more after dinner tonight?"

"Splendid," she said.

"And I'll come up with a better idea," promised
Alfie. "You'll be here all afternoon and make certain
nobody else gets into the house?"

"All afternoon," Sister John told him firmly.

"Good. See you later then."

After hearing that a Mr. Ianicelli had penetrated their
defenses Sister Ursula became unusually subdued; one
could almost say he turned docile. He allowed Sister
John to tuck and baste him into skirt and veil and then
to walk him up and down the hall once. When he was
refused a kitchen knife—to protect himself, he said—he
swore only once, feebly. He didn't even complain when
Sister John announced they would hold afternoon
prayers in his room to acquaint him with the rituals of
their order, and he listened almost humbly as Sister
John read in a stern, declamatory voice, ". . . O Lord
deliver my soul from wicked lips and from a deceitful
tongue. . . ."

At five o'clock Sister John had just discovered a
spinning wheel in the basement and was adding this to
her inventory when Sister Hyacinthe came to tell her
that for the past hour a child had been watching her
from behind a tree at the edge of the garden. She had
been carefully transplanting her herbs, she said, and it
was making her nervous to be watched.

"I wonder . . ." said Sister John thoughtfully. "I wonder if that could be Alice. Did you speak to her?"

"She doesn't want me to know she's there. I'm not supposed to see her."

"Let's get the suitcase," said Sister John and, with notebook and holland cloths in hand, led the way to the preserve closet. Noting the piles of money naked and unprotected she unfurled her dustcloths and covered them, leaving them looking rather like loaves of bread rising on the shelves. Carrying the empty suitcase, she headed upstairs and through the kitchen to the garden. "Alice?" she called. When there was no response she turned to Sister Hyacinthe. "Which tree?"

"The big oak near the path into the woods."

Sister John set out alone, tiptoeing with the suitcase in hand. She found the child pressed to the tree like a windblown leaf, too shy even to lift her head; when Sister John gently pried her loose the girl promptly burst into tears. Sister John was not dismayed: she understood that for Alice this was a nervewracking venture into the unknown.

"Alice?" she said gently.

"Yes'm," the child gasped, wiping her nose with a dirty hand.

"This is your suitcase."

Alice stopped sniffling and looked up at Sister John. Sister Hyacinthe, joining them, saw an uncommonly plain child with ragged blond hair and small buttoned-up features, but when Alice wrenched her gaze from Sister John to the suitcase her eyes suddenly blazed. She made no move to touch the suitcase but a look stirred in her face like the first ripples of wind in a pond; the prim mouth softened, the sun rose in her eyes. Alice had met with bliss.

"Take it," Sister John said, watching her. "Take it and come back tomorrow. I think perhaps we can find a few small things to put into it."

Alice received ownership with dignity. A furtive little smile tugged at her lips as she struggled off toward the path with the suitcase banging against her thin legs. A moment later she vanished into the woods.

"That," said Sister John unnecessarily, "was Alice."

As the afternoon waned the sky began to fade to the color of dull pewter. A hot, sickly breeze sprang up to flutter the drooping leaves of the trees, a few drops of rain fell and the earth became very still. "Blowing up a storm," said Sister Hyacinthe as they dined on mushroom omelet.

"I wonder if we have candles."

"Yes, in the drawer. A whole box."

The wind suddenly burst around the corner of the house with a roar, and Sister Hyacinthe, hurrying to the window, saw the privet hedge bend almost double and the elms' leaves turn white as the wind whipped them inside out. In the wake of the wind came rain: great sheets of it beating against the glass. Through it Sister Hyacinthe saw lightning flash and raced the thunder back to her omelet, saying crossly, "I suppose this means that Brill and Naomi and Alfie won't come over tonight."

"I think you're right," Sister John said, nodding. "This will be a wonderful chance for some quiet reading, a little more inventory, a little sewing. The world has been very much with us, Sister Hyacinthe, but I think we'll be left entirely alone this evening."

Which, as it turned out, proved that Sister John could be wrong on occasion, too.

9

The events that Sister John later referred to as their haunting began about nine, after the storm had left every tree and shrub dripping, and the earth sodden. Quite suddenly—and without reason, for the wind had long since died away—the lights went out. Sister John, reading Brill's book in the living room, was left hanging in the middle of a sentence. Sister Hyacinthe, seated on the floor grinding slippery elm bark for breakfast, gave a small gasp and said, "The lights have gone out."

"Hey," shouted Sister Ursula from upstairs, "the lights have gone out."

Rising, Sister John moved to the bottom of the stairs and called, "We'll be up with candles in a few minutes." She asked Sister Hyacinthe in which drawer the candles could be found, and then groped her way through the passage to the kitchen table. She unearthed the flashlight as well as the candles and, thus armed, returned to the living room to discover Sister Hyacinthe kneeling behind a chair. "Heard something outside," she whispered. "A noise."

"Nonsense, that's your imagination again," Sister

John told her firmly. "Get off the floor, Sister Hyacinthe—you really must, you look like a Thurber animal crouched there—and help drip tallow into saucers for candleholders."

Sister Hyacinthe reluctantly stumbled to her feet. One flickering candle did little to banish the darkness; it sent menacing shadows leaping up the walls but left the remainder of the high-ceilinged room in darkness. The smell of hot tallow filled the room as Sister John bent over saucers and distributed hot wax. When several candles were rooted and upright Sister Hyacinthe carried them to the mantel and placed them there in a row. As she turned, her mouth dropped open, she drew in her breath sharply, extended a trembling finger toward the window and screamed.

Following her glance of horror, Sister John looked at the window and saw a face peering at them through the glass, a face illuminated by a shimmering otherworldly light, floating in mid-air without neck or shoulders, eyes deep-set and burning, every seam of its waxen flesh outlined and shadowed by the luminous unearthly light. It was the face of a man in torment. For a long moment he stared through the glass at them while they stared back at him in astonishment and then, as suddenly as he had come, he disappeared like marsh mist.

"You—s-s-saw it?" gasped Sister Hyacinthe, clinging to the mantel.

Sister John looked down at her hands and saw that her knuckles were white where she gripped the candles. She thought, "How odd."

She must have spoken the words aloud because Sister Hyacinthe cried, "Odd! It was terrible!"

Sister John shook her head. "There is no such thing

as a ghost, Sister Hyacinthe, although I must admit—"
She stood up, flashlight in hand. "I think we'd better go
up and hide Sister Ursula immediately."

"No one can hide from ghosts," pointed out Sister
Hyacinthe despairingly. "I'm not stirring, I won't—"
She stopped as a low moaning sound reached them
from outside, a sound as melancholy and plaintive as
the cry of a lost child. Without comment Sister John
headed for the stairs with flashlight and candles. "Don't
leave me!" gasped Sister Hyacinthe, and tore herself
from the mantel to follow.

Upstairs they found Sister Ursula looking pale and
shaken, half out of bed and his coif askew. "Are we being attacked?" he asked. "What the hell's going on
down there?"

"Into the closet," Sister John told him, and after one
glance at her stern face he tottered across the floor to
the closet, the flashlight was thrust into his hands and
he was abandoned there.

"Now we'll double-check all the doors and windows," Sister John said.

"I w-w-wish w-w-we'd done it first," stammered Sister Hyacinthe.

"We didn't," pointed out Sister John, and returning to
the top of the staircase came to an abrupt stop.

"What is it?" whispered Sister Hyacinthe, bumping
into her.

Sister John blew out her candle, leaving only the
flickering candles in the living room to illuminate the
downstairs hall. "Listen."

That was when Sister Hyacinthe heard the footstep
on the porch. It was a heavy step, followed by the protest of rotted wood beneath it and then the unmistakable

sound of chains dragging slowly across the porch. Another step was taken and the rattle of chains repeated. Sister Hyacinthe clung to Sister John, shivering. Even Sister John, who didn't believe in ghosts, felt a chill run from the base of her spine to her scalp. The country silence had been profound, almost bottomless following the storm, and these unnatural sounds went beyond the rational to awaken ancient primitive terrors of the night. She, too, stood waiting.

The knock when it came was a soft tap on the door.

"He'll come in now," said Sister Hyacinthe, and swayed alarmingly against Sister John.

A moan rose and fell, like a dog whimpering at the door, and then the dragging steps were heard again, this time in retreat, and silence fell.

"We *must* check the doors," said Sister John resolutely, and grasping Sister Hyacinthe by the arm helped her down the stairs. "Sit," she told her, "while I make certain the door to the cellar is locked."

"Cellar!" cried Sister Hyacinthe in an anguished voice. "Oh, I couldn't bear it if they came up through the cellar, all dead and cobwebby. It's the spirit of the dead haunting us, Sister John, even Alfie said that people must have died violently here."

If Sister John heard her she gave no evidence of it; she was feeling her way through the dark to the cellar door. She turned the key in the ancient lock, listened a moment for sounds from the basement and, returning to Sister Hyacinthe, became aware of gentle tapping sounds at the dining-room window.

"This is ridiculous," she said angrily. "What's more it's undignified. Sister Hyacinthe, we're going to resume our places in the living room, light all the candles we have and sit there if the whole house falls down around us. *Someone* has a very macabre imagination."

"We'll go mad," pointed out Sister Hyacinthe. "They'll find us here tomorrow and we'll be nothing but gibbering idiots."

"Well, don't sound so pleased about it," Sister John said crossly, lighting more candles and distributing them around the room. "I think your imagination is a little macabre, too. Try having more faith, Sister Hyacinthe."

Sister Hyacinthe gave her a bleak, reproachful glance but was silenced. Candles lighted, Sister John took her place in the chair that faced both sets of windows, brought Brill's book to her lap and bent her attention to it. She read: *Terror stalks the streets at night in any urban community in America but even more corroding is the expectation of terror, with its resultant inhibiting factors: loss of faith in humanity, the lost spontaneity of a casual walk to the newsstand at midnight. Unfortunately, even locked inside an apartment there is no feeling of real security. There remains the dread of a hand at the window, a knock on the door. . . .*

Sister John firmly put the book down and reached instead for the Office of the Blessed Virgin. Across from her Sister Hyacinthe sat stiff as a poker in her high-backed chair, her eyes riveted on Sister John. She said through clenched teeth, "I think we're being watched, Sister John."

"I'm sure we are," said Sister John, nodding. "If I were a ghost I should feel quite snubbed if no attention was paid. I'm sure they—he—can see us quite clearly through the window."

"I wonder if my coif is straight."

"Quite straight, Sister Hyacinthe."

The shutter in the kitchen window banged hard against the house and something fell with a thud against the back door. The moaning began again, followed this time by soft, ghostly music.

"Harp," said Sister John in a pleasant voice. "I always did enjoy harp music."

"*Must* we sit here like this?" protested Sister Hyacinthe.

"Yes, it's good for our characters," replied Sister John, and turning to her book of office began to read aloud in a clear voice, " 'The Lord is protector of my life: of whom shall I be afraid? Whilst the wicked draw near against me to eat my flesh—' "

"Please," begged Sister Hyacinthe.

"—Mine enemies that trouble me have themselves been weakened . . ." She stopped, aware of a soft, luminous light floating past the window and when she resumed reading her voice was louder. ". . . and have fallen. If armies in camp should rise up against me, in this will I be confident—"

"What's happening?" asked Sister Hyacinthe, closing her eyes.

"The face is at the window again. No, no, don't look, Sister Hyacinthe."

The face dimmed and vanished and they sat in silence, waiting, but aside from one loud and piercing scream in the vicinity of the dining-room window there was a cessation of movement and sound outside. Sister John watched ten minutes crawl past on her watch and put down her book. "I think it's over."

Sister Hyacinthe warningly shook her head. "Not yet," she said, listening, but the voices they heard approaching the house now were normal voices in conversation. A moment later the screen door creaked and Alfie called, "Sister Hyacinthe, Sister John, are you all right?"

"A blessed sound," murmured Sister John, and rose from her chair to unlock the door.

When she opened it she found Brill, Alfie and Naomi staring at her in astonishment. "We heard a scream about ten minutes ago," said Naomi. "We came as fast as we could. What's happened to your lights?"

"Aren't the lights out everywhere?"

Brill shook his head. "Even the street light on Fallen Stump Road is shining." They stood brandishing flashlights, looking wonderfully alive, strong and capable in their dripping rain slickers and boots. "Is something wrong?"

"A great deal wrong," Sister Hyacinthe told them eagerly.

"*Was* wrong," corrected Sister John. "You have flashlights—could we all take a look around before going inside?"

They tramped through the wet grass to the rear where they discovered that the electric wires had been severed at the point where they entered the house. Someone had even taken the time to wrap up the slack and coil it neatly over a wisteria vine. "An orderly mind," pointed out Sister John. They also found that a truck had recently been parked at the service driveway down near Fallen Stump Road, for the mud still bore the imprint of wide-track double tires. Several footprints led into the tall grass before they disappeared.

"Okay, what happened?" asked Brill, turning to Sister John.

In a matter-of-fact voice she told him, and Alfie

shocked Sister Hyacinthe by remarking with admiration that it was a damned clever trick and he would like to meet whoever thought of it. She did not, however, abandon her illusions of the supernatural until Naomi spotted the tiny electronic device on the tree by the dining room window. It was attached to the trunk by means of a suction cup, and when she pulled it away it wheezed and gasped out one last feeble bar of harp music.

"They forgot to take this one away," said Sister John grimly. "Transistorized, too, no doubt?"

"Obviously they didn't know what they were up against," Naomi told her in an awed voice. "They thought you'd run screaming from the house, and then they'd go inside and look for Sister Ursula."

"Sister Ursula! Oh dear, we've forgotten all about him," exclaimed Sister John, startled. "We tucked him into the secret passage more than an hour ago."

They hurried inside and up the stairs to Sister Ursula's room, where Sister Hyacinthe fumbled for the hidden lever and slid back the wall of the closet. "Sister Ursula?" she called.

Alfie shone his flashlight on an empty landing, and spoke the obvious. "He's gone."

Sister Hyacinthe and Sister John exchanged horrified glances. "Down the *stairs*?"

"To the basement?" gasped Sister Hyacinthe.

Flashlights were focused, and in single file they descended the narrow secret staircase but there was no sign of Sister Ursula, either on the steps or collapsed in a heap at the bottom. Sister John pressed against the preserve closet wall and passed through it first, which gave her a moment to check the money. She found it still intact under the dustcloths. By the time the others joined her, however, there was no doubt but that Sister Ursula was somewhere in the basement, for they could all hear the sounds of joyous singing from another room.

They found him in the wine cellar, seated on the floor with his coif in his lap and his long veil tucked rakishly over one ear. Four empty bottles stood in a circle around him; he clutched a fifth to his bosom and with eyes closed and mouth open lustily sang, "There was a young virgin named Cherry . . . with whom we made very very merry . . ."

Sister John sighed and shook her head. "How tedious this is going to be," she said. "Tomorrow we'll not only have to call the electric company and the police, but before we do anything else we'll have to do some serious work on strengthening Sister Ursula's character."

Alfie grinned. "It certainly gives you a busy day."

"I told you," Sheriff McGee said the next morning, standing in the rear garden and staring resentfully at the house. He chewed irritably on the stub of his Sani-Smoke cigar, which muffled his voice but not his indignation.

"Told us what?" asked Sister John.

"Three of you here alone is asking for trouble. I warned you."

"No, I don't think you did," said Sister John, considering his statement judiciously.

His glance was cold. "I've been making inquiries and there's no doubt about it, your house has a very bad reputation in the neighborhood. A real ghosthouse, people call it. Strange lights now and then. Noises. Am I right, Al?"

Al Carson from the power and light company glanced down from the porch roof and shrugged. "All I know is, no ghost put these wires out of order. A knife did it, and I never heard of a ghost carrying a knife."

The sheriff didn't appear to appreciate this. "I'll take a look inside the house."

"But the ghost didn't *go* inside," pointed out Sister John.

"Mercifully," added Sister Hyacinthe.

"Just the same I'll have a look around."

"Not," said Sister John firmly, "until Sister Ursula has been told that a man is coming into the house. She was about to have a bath, wasn't she, Sister Hyacinthe?"

"I hadn't planned on going into the bathroom," said the sheriff.

"Nevertheless please wait until Sister Hyacinthe has alerted Sister Ursula. She's easily upset."

"*You* don't seem to be," the sheriff said suspiciously, as Sister Hyacinthe hurried toward the house.

"Sister Ursula is nearly eighty," she told him shamelessly, "and although fortunately she was, er, dead to the world during the events of last evening, nevertheless the sudden appearance of a man would definitely frighten her. She's lived in cloister for years."

"Why doesn't it scare you too?" asked the sheriff, chewing on this subject like a cud.

Sister John's glance was impatient. "I don't see why that fact interests you. I'd always assumed that a policeman's job is to prevent women from being frightened, not to analyze why they're not."

With this remark the battle was joined, the sheriff staring hard at Sister John and she returning his glance calmly, thereby earning another black mark against herself by refusing to be outstared. His glance fell first and a dark flush stole over his neck; he turned on his heel and stalked toward the house, dropping his dead cigar in the grass.

Sister John picked up the cigar stub and was about to follow him when she saw Al Carson shaking his head at her. "Shouldn't have talked back to him," he said sorrowfully.

"I didn't really. What's the matter with him, anyway, is he bilious?" asked Sister John. "When we first met he threatened us with handcuffs and jail."

Al Carson nodded. "You're probably too Catholic for him . . . I know I'm too black for him. If someone's too poor he gets mean and if they're too rich he gets nasty. He also likes men to have short hair and women to stay in their place. And he *hates* change."

"He must be a very lonely man."

Al snorted. "The hell he is. Not even the smoke from those fancy Sani-Smoke cigars of his keep his cronies away."

"How do you happen to know so much about him?"

He winked. "We blacks know all the things you've always wanted to know about white people but were afraid to ask."

Sister John shook her head incredulously, picked up her skirts and hurried into the house where she found the sheriff standing unsupervised at the door to the pantry. "Where's Sister Hyacinthe?" she asked, taken aback at finding him alone.

He said in a kindly voice, "I really don't know, ma'am." The change in his manner was startling; he looked almost serene, as if a religious experience had happened to him between the garden and the house. "I think I'll be moving along now, Sister, there's a good bit of work waiting downtown but I'll see to it that a police car patrols Fallen Stump Road at least once during the night. That way if there's any more hanky-panky—Probably teen-agers," he added, moving toward the door.

"Teen-agers?"

"Yeah, teen-agers. Halloween stuff."

"But this is July," pointed out Sister John.

"Maybe so," he said, standing outside and studying the back of the house, "but kids these days are pretty advanced. Who boarded up the pantry window there?"

"Alfie."

The sheriff shook his head. "Troublemakers, those kids. Outsiders. Wouldn't be at all surprised if they aren't behind the whole thing." With this announcement he strolled toward his patrol car, climbed inside and drove away.

Al Carson had gone, too, but the refrigerator was humming again as she returned to the kitchen. She continued upstairs in search of Sister Hyacinthe and found her in Sister Ursula's room. Sister Ursula was also there, lying in bed with towels covering his head.

"I couldn't persuade him to hide," explained Sister Hyacinthe. "He says he died sometime during the night. He says he can't move and his head is bursting."

"It's a hang-over," Sister John said sternly, "and just what he deserves."

The towels trembled and a jaundiced eye appeared among the folds. "That's a very un-Christian remark, I think you're monsters of piety, both of you. Here I am, at least ten martinis behind since getting shot, and you begrudge me a little wine. Damn good wine, too."

"Yes, 1912 and expensive," said Sister John. "We had a sheriff downstairs a moment ago, and you were supposed to be in the bathroom. If he'd come up to look around—" She walked to the door and stopped to look back at him, saying indignantly, "I don't think I've met anyone with such a low frustration tolerance. Or," she added, "such a dim talent for survival."

She left, and Sister Ursula said reflectively, "I think she's angry."

"Basically, yes," agreed Sister Hyacinthe.

Sister John found Brill waiting downstairs for her. It was his day off from bean picking, he said, and he had come to ask if they had any chores or errands that needed doing. Sister John thanked him with feeling and sent him off with a shovel to reinstate the mailbox on Fallen Stump Road. He not only succeeded in making it vertical but presently returned to ask what name to paint on it.

"Sisters of St. Tabitha," she said.

"Then here's a letter for you," he said, producing an envelope. "The postman happened to drive past while I was working."

Sister John glanced at the address on it and excitedly lifted her voice. "A letter, Sister Hyacinthe," she called. "It's postmarked the day we left the abbey."

Sister Hyacinthe hurried down and seated herself on the bottom stair; only then did Sister John open it, reading it aloud to Brill as well as Sister Hyacinthe.

"I know you will be pleased to hear," wrote the abbess, "that this morning's mail—which arrived shortly after your departure—brought a letter to us from our motherhouse in Switzerland. Dear Mother Therese, from whom we have had so many inspiring and helpful letters, has replied at last about Mr. Moretti's legacy. She writes that, knowing the difficulties that have beset us here, she wishes us to have all the benefits of the legacy since their vineyards have been blessed with three fine years. They will not hear of our sharing any proceeds from the gift with them. . . .

"And so, dear Sister John," continued the abbess, "you see how important your mission is, and how we rely on you. I have sent you out into the world with Sister Hyacinthe, not only to learn about the world, but also to learn what contribution we can best make to it for the glory of God. I place the decision entirely in your hands."

Sister John put down the letter. "In my hands," she whispered. "Oh, how wonderful, perhaps we can even do something for the migrant workers."

"Like what?" asked Brill, amused.

Her eyes had begun to sparkle. "I haven't given it much thought yet but with so much scope—It's not only the house, you know, there are the furnishings, some of them valuable, I'm sure. However"—she brushed this aside impatiently—the only thing I can do for them—right now—is organize a little trip into town tomorrow, like a party, and give the children a cultural experience."

"You'll frighten them," said Brill flatly.

"Not if you help persuade them and their parents. Sister Hyacinthe and I can bake cookies this afternoon and you and I can take them over this evening after they've come in from the fields. You'd help me talk to them, wouldn't you?"

"Of course," said Brill, watching her with a smile.

"We'll make sugar cookies," she said, turning to Sister Hyacinthe.

"We certainly have enough sugar," said Sister Hyacinthe.

"We'll make them now," said Sister John, and led the way into the kitchen. "Have you seen any cookie sheets, Sister Hyacinthe?"

"Yes," said Sister Hyacinthe, "but I don't care to go in the pantry and walk on all the sugar spilled on the floor."

"I didn't spill any," Sister John said, joining her at the door to the pantry. "You must have, Sister Hyacinthe."

"No, I didn't. I carried three jars to the basement yesterday but I didn't spill any. I went into the pantry last night to get slippery elm bark and there wasn't any sugar on the floor, and I've not been in the pantry today at all."

"Nor have I," said Sister John, frowning at the grains scattered across the dark floor. "It's slippery to walk on, and of course it attracts ants."

"Who'd want to steal powdered sugar?" asked Brill. He knelt down, stabbed it with a damp finger and carried the finger to his lips. "Ech," he said, making a face. *"Aaah."* He spat it out in distaste. "That's not sugar."

"Not sugar!" echoed Sister John. "It has to be sugar, we're going to make cookies with it. Unless of course something else spilled." She glanced up and down the shelves in search of something else but found nothing remotely resembling sugar.

"Let's be scientific about this," urged Brill. "Get me a spoon and show me where you think this came from."

"One of those last three jars on the top shelf," said Sister John, reaching up to grasp one. "This," she said, handing it to him. "We moved the others to the preserve closet."

He carried the jar to the kitchen table and took the spoon that Sister Hyacinthe offered him. Opening the container he scooped out a spoonful, studied it, sniffed it, then carried a few grains to his lips and tasted it. "Same stuff," he said, "and definitely not sugar. Has a weird aftertaste."

"Oh dear, the cookies," sighed Sister John.

"I wonder what it is," Brill said speculatively. "I can't think what it could be unless it's—but it couldn't be, it would be too wild. Crazy."

"What would be crazy?"

"Dope," he said bluntly. "It could, of course, be some kind of fancy rat poison but I wouldn't be at all surprised if this isn't some kind of drug."

"Drug?"

"I've got a friend who could run a test on it. Very discreetly, you understand. Good Lord, you could spend the rest of your lives in jail if this is what I think it is."

Sister John looked incredulous and then shocked. Sister Hyacinthe, on the other hand, brightened. "How Alfie's going to hate having missed this," she said. "His dearest dream come true."

"Yes, but what could Mr. Moretti have been thinking of," protested Sister John. "And how are we to bake our cookies?"

"More to the point," said Brill, "is who's been in your kitchen and found the damn stuff, spilling it in the meantime."

Sister John stared at him in astonishment. "Oh dear."

"Oh dear *what?*"

"Sheriff McGee was in the house. Right here in the kitchen, actually, but surely a sheriff, no matter how disagreeable—"

"Think. Anyone else?"

"There was the power and light man but he didn't come into the house at all, did he, Sister Hyacinthe?"

Sister Hyacinthe shook her head. "He just came to the back door, said he could see the problem without coming inside but he wanted me to know the Marines had landed—that's how he put it—and then he asked who could have cut the wire. I said we didn't know."

"Could one of your ghosts have sneaked in during the haunting last night?"

Sister John shook her head. "The doors were locked, and as you can see the pantry window's still boarded over."

"But Sheriff McGee did come in?"

"Yes, I found him standing near the door to the pantry."

"The pantry again," said Brill.

"He looked very happy. Not at all disagreeable, which, considering how angry he'd been several moments earlier, was a very pleasant surprise."

"The pantry made Mr. Ianicelli happy, too," pointed out Brill. Seeing Sister John struck silent by this, and suddenly thoughtful, he said, "Look, how much money have you? Frankly I suggest you buy about fifty pounds of sugar in one hell of a hurry."

"We don't need fifty pounds for cookies," said Sister Hyacinthe.

Sister John, however, understood him. "You're thinking we should replace this—this mystery ingredient—right away? It's that serious?"

Brill nodded. "It scares me, frankly. It would scare you, too, if you knew what I'm thinking. I don't have Alfie's kind of mind, which is positively Machiavellian, but in New York State the laws are rugged for possession of drugs, and Sheriff McGee doesn't *like* you."

"Doesn't understand us," Sister John corrected gently.

"Then hide the stuff until we can find out what it is and what to do with it. McGee must have taken some of it away with him, and it boggles the mind what that can mean. He'll probably have it tested tonight or tomorrow, and as long as it's here in your pantry—"

Sister John nodded. "Your point is made."

"Good. Sister Hyacinthe and I will drive out for some sugar now. She'll never manage fifty pounds of it alone so I'll go with her, and while we're gone I suggest you lock all the doors and hide the stuff somewhere in the cellar. Don't tell either of us where you hide it, either. I'll keep several tablespoons of it for analysis."

Sister John nodded.

"And don't be alarmed if we're gone awhile. We may have to spread our purchases between two towns."

"To conceal what we're up to," Sister Hyacinthe said, nodding with enthusiasm. "It's all right, Sister John, isn't it?"

"Of course," said Sister John, sighing. "But such a nuisance."

When they had gone, with Sister Hyacinthe driving—
she didn't envy Brill the experience—Sister John bun-
dled up the last three jars and carried them downstairs
to join the others in the preserve closet. Placing them on
the shelf, she surveyed the collection dubiously, then sat
down on an up-ended pickle barrel to think where to
conceal ten five-pound jars of trouble. She felt a little
jaded, for it did seem as if one thing after another had
been happening, but this in no way dimmed her faith:
she knew that God would presently reveal His purpose
in sending them here. "We have, after all, been here
only four days," she told Him aloud, "and I'm in no
way discouraged by this puzzle but if you could send a
little more enlightenment—direct my attention in the
proper direction—I'd certainly appreciate it. As you
know, we've been living very simply at St. Tabitha's
and we lack worldly experience."

The problem for the moment remained where to hide
the containers. She rose and walked into the storage
room, where they had found the water turn-off, and began lifting holland covers. A cedar chest she discarded
as too obvious; an old piano attracted her briefly but
the idea of anything illicit or poisonous remaining in the
house began to feel increasingly distasteful to her. The
money in the well was obviously theirs, but although
she did not care to follow this to its logical conclusion
she could not feel that this mysterious substance belonged to them, too.

The money in the well . . . If no one had peered into
the well during all those years then obviously the well
could prove an equally successful place for concealing
ten large glass jars. Somewhere she remembered seeing
a pile of burlap bags and found them under the cellar

stairs. She placed five jars in one bag, five in another, secured them with rope and disobeying Brill's stern injunction to remain in the house she carried them out, one by one, to the garden. Before lowering them down the well she strolled casually about the yard, just to make sure that Alice was not behind a tree or Mr. Ianicelli lurking behind the barn, and then knotted them to the chain, lowered it and inserted a stick once more in the wheel to keep the two bundles above water level. Following this she found herself somewhat tired and breathless, and repaired to the front steps to rest. She was still there when Mr. Armisbruck's van returned. Brill was driving this time and Sister Hyacinthe looking mutinous.

As Brill climbed out of the van she heard him say, "But you're not supposed to blow your horn at every car on Main Street. In the first place you're not supposed to drive that fast in town, and in the second place—"

"But I would have hit them if they hadn't gotten out of my way," protested Sister Hyacinthe. "And how could they know I was coming if I didn't blow the horn?"

He faced her, hands on his hips. "How old are you, Sister Hyacinthe?"

She thought a moment. "Thirty-four."

"Well, you make me feel middle-aged, that's what's so infuriating. I've never seen such driving in my life."

Sister John rose and went forward to intervene. "Did you find sugar?"

He nodded. "Forty-five pounds, although if we'd had an accident—a very strong possibility, you know—

that's a hell of a lot of powdered sugar to spill over the thruway, let alone explain."

"I prayed for you," Sister John told him reassuringly. "Shall we get to work now?"

Brill went off to telephone his mysterious friend who might, with persuasion, test the mysterious substance that had occupied their pantry, and Sister Hyacinthe and Sister John went to work filling identical glass jars with genuine sugar. When the pantry had been restored to respectability it was lunchtime and they decided to bring Sister Ursula downstairs.

"Because," explained Sister John, "it will do him a great deal of good to get out of his room, and if the stairs don't tire him too much he might want to watch us bake cookies."

"Why?" asked Sister Hyacinthe skeptically.

"It's wholesome," pointed out Sister John. "It may recall his childhood to him."

Sister Ursula agreed with alacrity that he would like to lunch downstairs, and leaning on the two of them he presently arrived in the kitchen and sat down to catch his breath. He looked white, and it was obvious that he badly needed a shave, but as Sister Hyacinthe remarked, from the back he looked just like a nun. His disposition, which had improved at a change of scene, suffered a setback when he confronted rose hip soup, sliced cheese and bread, but after a few disgruntled remarks about tree bark one day and roses the next he ate with appetite. He even remained in the kitchen for the cookie-making, and was the first to sample a cookie from the first of the four dozen they baked. After this he went upstairs carrying with him an ancient book from the living room, entitled *Life Among the Cannibals*. It was, said Sister Hyacinthe darkly, just one more symptom of his obsession over meat.

At half-past six Naomi's motorcycle roared up the drive with a hooded passenger clinging to her waist. The passenger dismounted, Naomi waved and roared off again, leaving a small, round-faced bespectacled young man peering at them from their bottom step. "Good evening," he said blinking. "I'm Marvin Coombs."

Marvin, it seemed, worked in a suburban pharmaceutical company and Naomi had driven down the thruway to pick him up at the gates. He was a chemist. He was also nervous and declined a cup of tea, saying that he would first prefer to find out whether he was visiting a house full of rat poison or full of dope. In the kitchen he removed his green-hooded windbreaker and unwound a khaki pack from his back and placed it on the table. "Are you really nuns," he asked solemnly, with a quick, sidelong glance at them, "or are you in disguise for my visit?"

Sister Hyacinthe and Sister John looked at each other in astonishment.

"You'd probably better not answer," he said nodding. "Much wiser not to, although if you don't mind a suggestion—"

"Yes?" said Sister John.

A little embarrassed he said, "I honestly think you've overdone it a little. Long skirts, the veil—nobody wears that stuff any more, you know. Excuse me if I've offended you but where's the sample I'm to test?"

Concealing her amusement, Sister John brought him the white powder in a saucer. He rolled it between his fingers, sniffed it and nodded. "I think it's flake all right—snow, coke—but I'll run a few tests and make sure."

After this mystifying remark he busied himself with bottles and test tubes, and the kitchen became quiet except for the sound of a fly buzzing in the window and the occasional click of Marvin's glass tubes as they touched. Before he had finished they could hear Alfie's voice approaching, and Sister Hyacinthe turned eagerly to the door, waiting to share in his reaction at missing the day's intrigues.

When he arrived, running up the steps and inadvertently slamming the screen door in Brill's face, his response was just what Sister Hyacinthe had expected: a blend of awe, horror and excitement. "What have you found?" he asked breathlessly. "What a day and I wasn't here!"

Marvin Coombs glanced up, found Brill's eyes and spoke to them. "Close the door," he said. "Lock it, too."

"That bad?" asked Alfie.

When the door was closed and locked Marvin gestured toward his test tubes. "It's cocaine," he said. "Very pure strain. The amount I've just tested—a spoonful—would cost fifty dollars on the retail market. I don't," he said earnestly, "want to know how much more you have. I'm corruptible, I'm an underpaid chemist with very expensive hobbies."

"What are they?" asked Sister Hyacinthe with interest.

"Photography, skin diving and women," he said, blinking at her. "Not necessarily in that order. Now if it's all the same to you I'd like to get out of here."

"But you haven't had dinner, have you?" asked Sister John.

"No, ma'am, but I'd just as soon not stay here a minute longer than necessary. It makes me nervous. Can Naomi take me back now?"

"I will," said Brill.

"You're not half so pretty," pointed out Marvin.

"But you were going to take the cookies to the farm with me," said Sister John, disappointed. "There they are, four dozen of them, and you promised."

Alfie sighed. "Okay, then, *I'll* drive Marvin back. *If* you'll make sure nothing else happens while I'm away."

"Perhaps you could bring back a razor," suggested Sister John. "I don't know whether you've noticed it but Sister Ursula badly needs a shave."

At this remark Marvin Coombs looked appalled, dropped a pencil and peered at her through his glasses. "You're all *men*?" he said in a shocked voice, and rolling up his pack he backed out of the room in a hurry.

"He thinks we're in disguise," Sister John told a mystified Alfie.

Alfie grinned. "I certainly wouldn't disillusion him for the world. I'll tell him you're members of the Mafia."

"Mafia," mused Sister John when he had gone. "Didn't that used to be another name for the Cosa Nostra?"

Brill nodded absently, his eyes on the saucer of cocaine in front of him.

"When I went into orders they were saying the existence of the Cosa Nostra was a myth, like the bogyman."

Brill heard her, glanced up and laughed. "You *are* behind the times, Sister John. Look, what do we do with this stuff that's left?"

"Flush it down the toilet," Sister John said, rising and taking it from him, but as she left the room there was a puzzled frown tugging at her brows and her eyes were thoughtful.

10

With a sense of great triumph Sister John had captured eight people for her excursion into Gatesville the next day, and she arose in the morning radiant with the joy of success. It had not been easy. On her side had been ranged only Alice, the cookies and Brill, while against her stood a rigid tradition of many years and a, to her, irrational panic. She felt it could not have been harder to enlist guides to accompany her among the headhunters of the Amazon, but six children had been offered up to her, with two adults to guard them: a young woman named Melida, and a toothless old man of seventy-seven called Uncle Joe.

"What about the cocaine?" asked Sister Hyacinthe as they faced each other at the breakfast table after prayers.

"I've thought about it," Sister John said, nodding. "This is our fifth day here, and you know we're honor bound to return the van to Mr. Armisbruck by the end of next week. The cocaine's hidden. I don't see how we can do anything at all about it until Sister Ursula is off our hands. We'll simply have to work with him every day to get him operative again.

"Operative?"

"It's a word from Brill's book, they use it a great deal in Washington. Brill says we can bypass Sheriff McGee when the right moment comes and call in the state police, but we can scarcely do that until we're prepared to throw open the house for a search. Our hands are not clean," she reminded Sister Hyacinthe sternly. "Sister Ursula remains a mystery, although I pray about this every day, and then there's the money." She sighed. "I'm not sure I could explain that to the police, either. If you'd like to count more of it while I'm in town, Sister Hyacinthe—"

"No thank you," Sister Hyacinthe said hastily.

"We're too busy today but I really think that on Monday we must rent a safe-deposit box and put the money in it. Last night I—" She dropped her voice dramatically. "Last night I carried the already counted batch into the storage room and hid it in the old piano there."

"Boysendorfer?"

"No, Steinway. I want you to remember where it's hidden. The rest is still in the preserve closet but I moved it out of sight by dropping it into the old wooden pickle barrel in the corner."

"Empty, I hope."

"Well, not now but if you mean are there pickles inside, no, although I have to confess there's still a strong smell of brine."

"Pickled money," said Sister Hyacinthe gaily. She was feeling surprisingly lighthearted because Sister John had not insisted on her joining the expedition: Naomi was going to drive the van. In turn Alfie had volunteered to take a few hours off from bean picking to protect Sister Hyacinthe, now that they were concealing not only Sister Ursula but fifty pounds of cocaine.

"But doesn't Mr. Eaton the farmer mind your missing so much time?" Sister John had asked him.

"He likes us," Alfie said, pleased. "Actually he's very sympathetic about the migrant workers but he has to make a living. He says if there was a really tough *enforced* law he wouldn't mind fixing up his shacks but it would take money none of the other farmers are spending and he couldn't deduct it as charity. The shacks are used only about six weeks out of the year, you see."

"And that's exactly where the solution lies," Sister John had said, nodding vigorously and at the same time looking mysterious.

Now she said to Sister Hyacinthe, "I know you won't let Mr. Ianicelli into the house again but I want you to remember that we seem to be surrounded by wolves in sheeps' clothing, all of them bent on coming inside."

"Yes, that's becoming obvious," pointed out Sister Hyacinthe, "but have you decided why?"

"An idea begins to take shape," Sister John told her, nodding.

"A deduction?"

"Yes, and although it bothers me a great deal to say this I feel you must regard any stranger with suspicion."

"I always have," Sister Hyacinthe said truthfully.

Sister John looked startled. "Yes, I suppose you have."

"I don't," said Sister Hyacinthe carefully, "trust people in general. I don't love them all, as you do, and look for God in them. I can't usually find God in them at all."

"It takes time," Sister John said, warmly patting her hand. "But for just one more week—heaven forgive me for saying it—I think it would be wise for you to continue being suspicious. *Then* you can try loving them." She arose and carried breakfast dishes to the sink. "I'll get ready now. . . . I plan to take the children through the five-and-dime store, show them the court house, the Catholic church and the supermarket and then buy each of them an ice-cream cone. In the meantime," she added, "there *could* be a letter from Mother Angelique today, in reply to my phone call. Watch for it, will you?" With this she picked up Sister Ursula's breakfast tray and vanished with it.

It was a motley-looking group that assembled in the garden an hour later, at nine o'clock. Uncle Joe was a black man bent almost double from rheumatism; he leaned heavily on Melida, who was blond, with a worn, once-pretty face turned passive from too many sterile hours. Alice led them, eyes shining, a small Joan of Arc in sneakers. Her five companions, none of them older than Alice, looked stupefied with terror. They were introduced as Moses, Rosebeth, Lucas, Harry and Carrie.

Almost at once Moses announced that he had to go to the bathroom and since he was too frightened to go alone Alice, Rosebeth, Lucas, Harry and Carrie insisted on accompanying him upstairs. They crowded into the bathroom together in spite of Sister John's protests, and while Moses attended to the call of nature the others examined the bathtub and made faces at themselves in the mirror.

"Rosebeth's got on her best hair ribbon," Alice confided to Sister John, "and Lucas is wearin' his pa's bow tie. Harry ain't got no tie but he's wearin' clean under-drawers special, an' Moses has socks on today and Carrie's wearin' beads."

"How nice," said Sister John, beaming at these revelations. "Are you quite finished now, Moses? Shall we go down and get into the car?"

En masse they left the bathroom, each of them wistfully stroking the banisters as they moved downstairs, where they collected in a knot and peered into the living room. "Don't touch—stand," Alice told them, and like puppies they stood.

"Okay," called Naomi, opening the doors of the van and waving to them. "In you go, sit on the floor and hold on tight."

Cars were obviously an oasis of the familiar after their brief glimpse into a Victorian mansion, for Harry promptly relaxed enough to hit Moses in the stomach. Sister John didn't see this because she was helping Uncle Joe into the seat up front but Sister Hyacinthe saw it and marveled again at Sister John's heroism. Once the children were stowed away in the back Melida and Sister John climbed in beside them, Naomi closed the rear of the van and inserted herself behind the wheel next to Uncle Joe. The van began to move, promoting a roar of squeals and giggles from the interior, and crawled down the driveway toward Fallen Stump Road.

Alfie said, looking after them, "Sister John really blows the mind, doesn't she?"

Gatesville was not a large town but it was a county seat. The era had long since passed when on Court Day citizens lined up to watch Judge Farley hit a spittoon at thirty feet with his tobacco juice, or when Jeb Pickering, weaving only slightly, made his way from South Main to North Main every morning, bowing and removing his hat at every pretty lady and sometimes at the statue of General Grant by the post office; Jeb was now banished to the Elmwood State Hospital, where eccentrics belonged. The original Gatesville—cluttered, colorful, easy-going—had turned into a suburban town whose virtues were preserved like an embryo in formaldehyde: these values were reflected in the elegance of the neo-Colonial gas stations, the long line of cedar-and-glass shops in the mall, the rather self-conscious antiquity of the old court house and the litter baskets painted pale blue each spring by the Cub Scouts. If the thoughtful eye found a certain blandness in the scene, that was the way Gatesville liked it. Dedicated to homogeneity, it had been at least twenty years since anyone had seen heterogeneousness on Main Street.

The van's arrival introduced heterogeneousness in one fell swoop. Since it was Friday, a major shopping day, there were a considerable number of people to observe the invasion of Gatesville by its migrant children. It elicited a number of benevolent smiles, for if there was one thing Gatesville prided itself on it was its liberal attitude toward the black and the poor, none of whom lived within its boundaries. The liberalness was of a particular generous quality because the town voted Republican so overwhelmingly at each election that no one could be labeled radical, no matter how liberal they dared to be: it was a situation that Sheriff McGee understood perfectly, and one which had returned him unerringly to office every four years.

There was a certain CARE-poster quality about the children as they climbed out of the van: Carrie began to suck her thumb, Alice clung to Sister John's skirts and Rosebeth began to sob quietly. Almost immediately Uncle Joe added to the confusion because it took nearly ten minutes to prise him out of the front seat and establish him on his feet. During this interval Moses announced that he had to go to the bathroom again, although once in motion he abandoned the idea; it was apparently a ploy with which he filled his idle moments. Uncle Joe's progress across Main Street to the five-and-dime store was slow, and stopped traffic for three blocks while he maneuvered between Sister John and Melida. Once in the store Sister John distributed dimes, only to discover that nothing could be purchased with a dime, and she began to wonder if she could afford the ice-cream treat later.

The visit to the five-and-dime store proved to be a success, however. The boys left clutching microscopic plastic trucks and the girls hair ribbons or jewelry; even Melida wore a faint wan smile. Once again they crossed Main Street, causing an even longer backup of cars as shoppers poured into town on late-morning errands. Reaching the court house they sprawled on the lawn while Sister John explained the functions of the law. This was received politely, the children occupied by their store purchases, but the driver of a passing truck shouted, "Right on, Sister!" From there they moved down the street to the Catholic church but since everyone appeared to be Baptist, Sister John's explanations were listened to with bewilderment. At last they crossed the street to the supermarket where Sister John planned to give the children a small lecture on food, nutrition and free enterprise.

It was the supermarket that proved their undoing.

Plastic toys and hair ribbons were all very well in their
place but for children who breakfasted on cold grits,
lunched on canned beans and saw meat and milk only
a few times a month, the sight of so much food produced far more reverence than any church, and a great
deal more excitement than toys in a discount shop. Not
even the music pouring softly through the walls could
equal the sight of aisle after aisle of shelves filled with
cans and boxes of food. They clustered around Sister
John and Naomi, urgently pointing and tugging, all except for Uncle Joe who backed against a deceptively
solid pyramid of canned corn (Weekend Sale 4/1.00).
The towering display of cans trembled, tilted and cas-
caded, can by can, to the floor.

One hundred cans of corn (4/1.00) caused a great
deal of noise and sent Uncle Joe to his knees. Melida
screamed and ran up the aisle to hide behind a special
weekend display of Picnic Pleasers, Naomi raced to
stop the cans from rolling all over the store and Sister
John tried to help Uncle Joe to his feet. Alice began to
cry softly. Moses announced in a loud voice that he had
to go to the bathroom, and strung to a new pitch of anx-
iety Carrie began to vomit.

It was a trying moment.

Into this circle of total confusion strolled Sheriff
McGee, not at all surprised to see them: news of their
arrival in town had reached him two minutes after they
parked their van. He had closely watched their progress
up and down Main Street, resenting very much their
squatting on the court house lawn, and still more their
holding up traffic. He was filled now with triumph at
finding them delivered to him like so many wiggling
fish in a net.

"All right, all right," he said, wading through the cans. "All right, that's enough, let's move along now. I'll handle it, Joe," he told a harassed store manager who arrived breathlessly from the nether regions. "You get somebody to clean up this mess and I'll get them out of your store."

"We can leave quite well by ourselves," Sister John told him, succeeding at last in propping up a dazed Uncle Joe. "He only backed up without looking behind him."

"Just come along," said the sheriff. "For Chrissake can somebody get this black kid a paper bag, she's upchucking all over my new boots."

Naomi, looking distraught, said, "Other people vomit in supermarkets and knock things over by accident."

"Yeah, well, they're taxpayers. Right now I'm arresting you all for disturbing the peace on a Friday morning in Gatesville."

"Arresting us for *what*?" gasped Sister John.

The manager said, "Oh, come on now, Bill, that's overdoing things a bit, isn't it? I'm not complaining."

"I didn't catch your name," Sister John told him happily.

"Epworth. And what's more, Bill—"

"What's more, they were disturbing the peace all up and down Main Street," said Sheriff McGee. "You give these people an inch and they'll take a mile, Joe. You want them in your store every day?"

Joe looked around him at a littered floor, gaping customers and terrified young faces. "Maybe they just got excited. I got no reason to kick them out, Bill. Their money's just as good as anybody's."

Sheriff McGee's laugh was contemptuous. "If they

have any! Well, *I've* got the right, and I know my Gatesville, how the hell d'ye think I stay in office?" To Sister John he said coldly, "Let's go."

"You're arresting *children*?" cried Sister John.

"Save your speeches for the court house," he said warningly. "All of you, no exceptions, move along."

11

For Sister Hyacinthe the first hint of anything unexpected came when six bedraggled children could be
seen approaching the house through the field of mustard
around two o'clock. She and Alfie were sitting on the
front steps waiting for the first glimpse of Mr.
Armisbruck's red van and assuming that a good many
bathrooms must have been visited to make the group so
late. "Look!" cried Sister Hyacinthe, and pointed.

Six heads, rising like flowers from the tall grass, in-
creased in height and presently gained shoulders and
waists as they mounted the sloping lawn. Behind them
limped only one adult figure in a pale flowered dress.
"That's Melida," said Alfie, shading his eyes against the
sun.

"But *walking*?" protested Sister Hyacinthe. "Where's
the van, and where are the others? They shouldn't be
walking, it's five miles from Gatesville."

"Maybe the van broke down," Alfie said, rising to his
feet.

Slowly the children made their way toward them and
stopped in a grim and silent line in front of them. Their

eyes were accusing. They had, after all, believed that
Sister John, with her long whispering skirts, her veil,
her shining face and smiling eyes, had possessed the
magic to protect them even when their parents had said
she did not. Melida, coming up behind them, nodded in
a civil manner, leaned over to take off her shoes and
said, "You better get down to the jail real quick, Alfie."

"Jail!" faltered Sister Hyacinthe.

"Yes'm, because Sister John's there, and Miss Naomi, and Uncle Joe's there, and that sheriff says we all
disturbed the peace of their day and he's a mean one.
No ma'am, we don't want to sit down, we just want to
get home, thank you, but somebody better go down before Sister John gets into any more trouble, and Miss
Naomi wants for you to call the—the BCLU I think it
is—"

"ACLU," put in Alfie.

"—and that sheriff, he put us in a room with a lady
who ain't no better than she should be, and Uncle Joe,
he's off by himself and that ain't good for him, seeing
as how he's a man who likes his folks close by him, and
what I want to know is, they let us go because Sister
John made such a fuss about the children, but who's to
get the rest of them out when they been arrested and
Sister John won't plead guilty?"

"She wouldn't, of course," Alfie said, staring in fas-
cination at a Melida who had never said more than yes
or no within his hearing.

"And," continued Melida, "Sister John's down there
threatening the sheriff and telling him she won't pay no
fine or even leave until he apologizes for arrestin' us
all."

"Oboy," said Alfie.

"Is that bad?" asked Sister Hyacinthe.

"Well, it's certainly *interesting*," admitted Alfie.

"And now we're going to go along home, seeing as how the children are tired," said Melida, "and afore the folks get to worrying about us if they ain't already."

"Yes," said Alfie. "And do you mind telling Brill what happened and get him over here in a hurry?"

"I surely will," Melida said with dignity, and herded the children toward the side of the house.

Just before they vanished Moses looked back and said over his shoulder bitterly, "We didn't get no ice cream neither."

The lunch that Sister Hyacinthe had made was eaten only by Sister Ursula; Alfie had brought his own with him and Sister Hyacinthe certainly had no appetite for food while Sister John languished in prison. Brill, hastily summoned from his bean-picking, arrived on Naomi's motorcycle and said he'd go at once to the court house to find out what had happened. "I warned her," he said mysteriously, and with a curt nod rode off. They did not see him again for eight hours.

At half-past five Bhanjan Singh walked up the driveway carrying a small suitcase. Sister Ursula had ventured downstairs for dinner because, as he put it evasively, it didn't seem the same upstairs without Sister John stopping in to pray over him at odd moments. Once established in the living room he discovered the Victrola and began issuing orders: "Does it work?" he asked. "See if you can find a handle. If there's a handle you insert it, wind it up and the damn thing plays without electricity. Are there phonograph records?"

Faced with preparing dinner and knowing her limitations, Sister Hyacinthe retired to the kitchen to do some research. From a pile of greens gathered in the woods she selected young nettle leaves, handfuls of red clover blossoms, dandelion greens and a number of fiddlehead ferns. From the refrigerator she extracted spinach and two onions, and seeing the collection grow she was pleased: after steaming the greens and sautéing the onions she would add two quarts of milk to make a soup teeming with vitamins and minerals. If anyone—it would be Sister Ursula, naturally—protested the clover blossoms she could insist it was spinach soup. Everyone ate spinach soup. For a main dish she would stuff comfrey leaves with cheese and breadcrumbs.

At that moment she heard the screen door slam and Bhanjan Singh's voice say, "Good afternoon please, everyone."

Brightening, Sister Hyacinthe dropped her apron and hurried into the hall to welcome him. He stood with the sun at his back, cordially beaming at them and bowing. "I had not planned to come until tomorrow," he said, "but I had a very strong intuitive feeling that I am needed today." He held out a letter. "I took the liberty in passing the mailbox to extract this envelope."

Sister Hyacinthe grasped the letter, read the words on the envelope and burst into tears. "It's j-j-just the letter Sister John was waiting for and now she's in prison, Bhanjan."

"It has already begun then," he said, nodding. "You must not lose faith: an eclipse is sometimes a great blessing. I wonder if you could tell me where to place my suitcase, please?"

* * *

There were three jail cells provided in the court house for unhappy souls in transit, and the first cell was occupied by two other women beside Sister John and Naomi. Uncle Joe sat alone in the second cell and passed the time praying in a loud voice while a gentleman with delirium tremens huddled in the third and complained loudly that Uncle Joe was sending green-haired angels into his cell. "Get them away," he shouted over and above Uncle Joe's solemn *Thy kingdom come, Thy will be done on earth as it is in heaven.*

Only Naomi was calm, giving invaluable legal advice to Sister John, whose indignation remained at a high pitch until the children were at last sent home with Melida. This took place around one o'clock, and only then did Sister John relax and turn her attention to her cellmates, remedying her previous oversight by announcing that she was Sister John of St. Tabitha's Abbey.

The girl lying on the lower bunk reading *Amazing Confessions* looked up and said sarcastically, "No kidding."

Sister John stared at her in astonishment; she was certainly no older than fifteen. "What on earth are you doing here, you poor child?"

The girl's glance was bored. "Shoplifting," she said. "A bum rap, and if Daddy doesn't come soon and get me out of this hellhole I'll raise bloody murder."

Taken aback, Sister John turned more hopefully toward the other woman, a neat young woman in sandals, bare legs and a cotton frock. The young woman put down her book and smiled. "I hoped we might meet presently," she said. "I see you're Benedictine—I'm Dominican."

"I beg your pardon?" said Sister John blankly.

"Dominican," repeated the young woman. "I'm working with drug addicts at the House of Hope. I'm Sister Isabelle Irwin."

"You're one of the new nuns!" gasped Sister John, and eagerly thrust out her hand. "How perfectly wonderful, there's so much I want to ask you, so much I want to hear. Oh, do sit down over here so we can have a long and serious chat."

"I'd love to," said Sister Isabelle.

"Take them away," screamed the man in the cell on their left, and on their right Uncle Joe haltingly finished reciting the 123rd Psalm and began on the 124th.

"First of all," began Sister John, and drew a deep breath . . .

"I don't appreciate clover blossoms in my soup," Sister Ursula said at dinner, predictably and with venom.

"There is a saying," Bhanjan Singh told him, "that could very well apply to you, my friend: He cackles often but never lays an egg. If you would observe yourself coolly and dispassionately you would see yourself as others see you. This could be far more crushing than clover blossoms in your soup."

"Besides, it's spinach soup," Sister Hyacinthe told him but was, on the whole, inclined to forgive him because she noticed how frequently he looked toward the door. She was edgy herself, impatient for Brill's return and mystified by his lateness. "Everyone leaves for Gatesville and disappears," she lamented.

When Brill returned at last it was nearly ten o'clock and he came alone. "I didn't see any of them but I've gotten things rolling," he said, throwing himself into a chair. "There'll be an American Civil Liberties lawyer at the sheriff's office at ten o'clock tomorrow. His name is Jason Horowitz and he's in New York tonight for a meeting, but I talked with him on the phone and he'll be here on the 9:22 Saturday train."

"They're going to spend a night in *jail*?" gasped Sister Hyacinthe. "Not only Sister John and Uncle Joe but an innocent young girl like Naomi?"

"Naomi won't mind," said Brill, and seeing Sister Hyacinthe's shocked gaze he explained, "She's been there before, in the sixties. Peace marches. Demonstrations."

"But Sister John has never been in jail," she reminded him.

Brill grinned. "No, but Sister John is engaged in a battle of wills with the sheriff, and is exploring the thought of martyrdom. It seems they could all come home if they paid a fine, pleading guilty, but Sister John refuses and Naomi agrees, and Uncle Joe can't leave and walk the five miles back so he's elected to stay, too. As a matter of fact, Melida was only too accurate: Sister John's gone even farther. She won't leave until the sheriff admits he discriminated against Melida, Uncle Joe and the kids."

"She could be there for years," protested Alfie. "Sheriff McGee isn't going to admit any such thing."

"She's on strike," breathed Sister Hyacinthe happily. "*Now* I understand."

"She's a nut," blurted out Sister Ursula. "It's all your influence; she'll turn into one of those militants yelling about peace and love. Sheer cussedness."

"Don't be silly, it's a matter of principle. I stopped in at the supermarket and talked to the manager, a guy named Epworth. He said it was perfectly obvious the sheriff's trying to scare the migrant workers away from coming into town again. Epworth's a good guy. When I left him at six he was packing bags of groceries to take to the migrant workers' camp. He said it was the least he could do, and where could he find them? I gave him directions."

"I suppose he's taking them steak," put in Sister Ursula bitterly.

"She's been praying," said Sister Hyacinthe, nodding. "When Sister John prays the most surprising things happen. Our electric water pump broke down in 1969 and Sister John prayed until she had blisters on both her knees."

"What happened?"

"Mr. Doermann came. He lives in Bridgemont Corners and builds windmills. He asked if he could put a free windmill on our property to show people how pretty they look and how much money they could save. He took care of all the expenses, including a new water pump. After he built the windmill Sister John prayed for *him* and he sold eleven."

Brill was staring hard at Sister Ursula as if seeing him for the first time. "Good Lord, you need a shave," he said. "Didn't anyone shave you last night? If someone looked in one of the windows and saw you sitting here we'd all be in the soup." To Sister Hyacinthe he said, "If you don't mind we'll all stay here with you tonight."

Five miles away, in the bowels of the court house, Sister John was saying earnestly, "So that's how I happen to be here but, my dear, you're not wearing a habit, is there anyone to speak for you? Does the sheriff know you're a religious?"

"Not yet," said Sister Isabelle blithely, "but someone will come for me because I telephoned and left a message. I live at Community House over in Gatesville Heights, and one of the priests will bail me out. You see, I was stupid enough to take one of the House of Hope addicts to visit her mother, except that it turned out to be her supplier, not her mother. The police were watching the house and when they broke down the door Agnes slipped five ounces of marijuana into my purse. A very hostile child. And so stupid of me! But I find it very difficult to think like an addict. They're not *themselves*."

"Like Sister Ursula," said Sister John, nodding.

"They can be very devious. Of course I should have waited until someone could go with me but I was impatient. I have to confess that we're all impatient, we want to change things. Other things, too."

"What other things?" Sister John asked eagerly.

"Well," said Sister Isabelle, looking at her challengingly, "I'm a member of the National Coalition of American Nuns now."

"There's a union?" gasped Sister John.

"We want to end the oppression of women in the church. There has to be more to sisterhood than teaching second grade, it's so unfair."

"Women's Lib," said Sister John, nodding.

Sister Isabelle looked at her in surprise. "You're a little more with it than I thought, Sister John. Of course Women's Lib but human liberation, too. Everyone!"

* * *

"So what *do* you kids want?" asked Sister Ursula, pressed into a chair upstairs and lathered for his first shave. "After five days here I'll admit you're not as peculiar as I thought at first. You're not wild-eyed radicals or deadbeats either, although this could be my weakened condition. What bugs me, though, is what *are* you? I can't figure you out."

"You're always looking for labels," said Brill. "That's your first problem."

"Well, how the hell do I know where you fit without them?" growled Sister Ursula. "You're really not too different from my nephew—"

"He has a nephew," crowed Alfie.

"—but he works in a bank, making a hundred and fifty bucks a week and he buys things. You know, things like color television—and you've heard of telephones, those instruments used for communication?"

"And for obscene calls," put in Alfie.

"—and he's got a Mustang now. You could have a Mustang, too."

"Nothing less than a Rolls-Royce would suit us," said Alfie solemnly.

"Well, what the hell motivates you? Christ, you've all had college educations and you're picking beans?"

"We're leftovers from the sixties," said Alfie. "Flotsam and jetsam."

"All that burning and marching you mean?"

"Yes, as well as a few assassinations and an undeclared war. We've been shot at and we've been clubbed and we've been arrested and we're tired, that's all. And the hell of it," said Alfie, waving the razor at him, "is that we were right about the hypocrisy and the corruption. It's terrifying to be right before you're even old enough to vote. It's so frightening most of us have given up and retreated to the sidelines to put ourselves together again."

Bhanjan Singh, seated cross-legged on the floor, nodded solemnly. "In the I Ching it says 'When grass is uprooted, what is attached to it is pulled up as well.' "

"But living in a bus and picking *beans*?" said Sister Ursula incredulously.

"The essential problem," said Sister John, speaking earnestly to Sister Isabelle, "is the migrant workers' always moving, never having a place to call home, a place to put down roots and go to school."

"And to vote," said Sister Isabelle, nodding.

"There should be—must be—some way to change that."

Sister Isabelle looked thoughtful. It was past midnight, the cells were quiet at last and the lights turned low. The young shoplifter had been bailed out by her father and the man with d.t.s had been taken off to a detoxification unit. Naomi dozed on the lower bunk nearby and Uncle Joe mumbled occasionally in his sleep in the next cell. "There's an experiment taking place in Florida," said Sister Isabelle at last. "I recently met one of the men involved in it. They're experimenting with settling the migrant workers into one place, one community exclusively theirs. It seems to be working, too. They've built their own homes and they're governing themselves and making the decisions . . . not without difficulty of course. Naturally it's heavily funded."

"Funded?"

"Money," said Sister Isabelle. "The government's

backing it—or was. OEO or HUD, I don't know—and the Ford Foundation was helping, too. Seed money."

"Seed money," echoed Sister John, struggling to master a new vocabulary.

"They pick crops within a certain radius of their community but they have their own homes now, simple as they are. Their own crops, too, and the children actually go to the same school all year."

"But that's marvelous!" exclaimed Sister John and then, in a thoughtful voice added, "Where can I find out more about it?"

"Why?" asked Sister Isabelle, startled.

"Because we have one hundred and fifty acres of land here."

"Really?" said Sister Isabelle. "You could do a lot with that, certainly, but it would need money, Sister John. Lots of money."

"How much?"

"Half a million? I don't know but I can give you the name and address of a man who knows all about it. He lives in New Jersey."

Sister John nodded. "I'd like that, Sister Isabelle, I'd appreciate it very much. Now tell me what OEO and HUD are, if you don't mind, and if you aren't terribly sleepy yet . . ."

"What's wrong with picking beans?" asked Alfie. "Growing things is real. People are real. Where are you going, Sister Hyacinthe?"

Sister Hyacinthe hesitated at the door. "I thought—I thought I might go downstairs, perhaps even out on the porch, and pray for Sister John. I can't bear the thought of her in jail all night."

Bhanjan Singh smiled at her gently. "She is not lost, you know. No man is lost who walks a straight path."

"I'll just remind God about her," Sister Hyacinthe said, and left.

"You were saying?" said Sister Ursula pointedly.

"Alfie's saying that a paycheck isn't enough," explained Brill. "A Mustang isn't enough. A split-level house in the suburbs is no longer enough."

"It's a matter of soul," added Alfie.

"You're copping out," Sister Ursula told him accusingly.

"No, I think we're into something real," contradicted Alfie. "There's certainly something damned real about pumping water by hand and growing vegetables without chemicals and patching things up to make them last. Bhanjan Singh has a saying: Observe that the things which are considered to be right today are those which were considered impossible yesterday. The things which are thought wrong today are those which will be esteemed tomorrow."

"Meaning what?" demanded Sister Ursula.

"We're working on tomorrow."

"Picking beans?"

"Not exclusively," Alfie said patiently. "You keep missing the point. I mean that when all the cars are rusted junk and the suburbs sterile and food in short supply and equipment scarce there have to be people who'll know how to put things together again. People who know how to live simply, without machines. And," he added, whipping the towel from Sister Ursula's shoulders, "I'll bet you don't believe we're right

about that either, but did you ever think oil would be
rationed?"

Downstairs Sister Hyacinthe wandered through the
dark rooms like a wraith, presently unlocking the front
door and venturing out into the coolness of the night.
The sky was bright with stars. The huge elm nearby had
captured a yellow crescent moon in its branches and
cradled it, filtering the pale silver light through its
leaves. In the shadows of the wisteria Sister Hyacinthe
knelt and prayed for Sister John. Her views might be
considered somewhat eccentric at St. Tabitha's but her
prayers were always sound and when she had finished
it was past midnight. She turned to go inside but the
moonlight caught at the gypsy in her and she hesitated.
Impulsively she unlaced her shoes, picked up her long
skirts and waded barefooted into the tall grass, laughing
at the shock of cold dew on her feet.

Delicious, she thought, and walked toward the rear
garden to greet her herbs. As she rounded the corner
of the house she found Mr. Quigley there in the act of
opening their garbage pail and she stopped, surprised.

Hearing her small intake of breath he, too, stopped in
mid-motion, his attitude guarded; they faced each other
in the pale white light of the moon.

Sister Hyacinthe said politely, "It's very nice of you
to come for our garbage."

"Yes," he said, staring at her intently.

"I'm not sure we can afford you, though. We save the
eggshells for the garden—for the lime in them—and
any cans we'll probably bury."

"Yes," he said.

"Although if you really need the work," she added generously, "by all means go ahead."

He responded at once, drew out the modest bag of garbage, replaced the lid and nodded to her. "Lovely evening," he said, and carrying the bag walked across the garden and disappeared into the woods.

12

In the morning Brill went off to meet the 9:22 train, taking with him the spare key to Mr. Armisbruck's van so that he could rescue it from its parking space on Main Street. Alfie stoically remained behind on guard duty; it was true that Bhanjan Singh knew some judo, he said, but the man was so persistently non-violent that he couldn't be trusted to fend off invaders. Obviously restless, he asked Sister Hyacinthe if she had anything for him to do.

"Yes," she said promptly, "you can scythe the front lawn and help me dry the mustard."

"But that's really Naomi's bag, she'd love doing it," he pointed out.

"Yes, but Naomi's in jail, and the morning's endless, and when Naomi's out of jail, God willing, there may not be time to dry mustard."

"Okay," he said, suddenly agreeable, and went off to look for a scythe.

It was a pleasant morning, cooler than yesterday, with a playful south wind ruffling the trees. Sister Ursula was dozing over his book on cannibals upstairs; Bhan-

jan Singh sat under a tree and meditated in the shade.
Alfie bared himself to the waist and began vigorously
scything a portion of their mustard-laden lawn while
Sister Hyacinthe followed behind him, bundling the
golden harvest into sheaves. Presently she went search-
ing for old window screens, found a collection of them
in the barn and carried them to the porch. Clumps of
blossoms were pressed between pairs of screens and
then placed across wooden sawhorses to dry in the
shade. "The rest of the mustard we'll have to dry inside
the house," she told Alfie, "and for that we'll need lots
and lots of paper bags."

He reluctantly put down the scythe and pulled on a
shirt. "What do we do with paper bags?"

"Hang them from the ceiling," she explained. "With
stalks of mustard tied upside down inside of them, of
course."

"Of course," he said, and helped her carry great piles
of greens into the kitchen where she distributed them
across the table, chairs and counters.

"Hooks," she said, removing a box from the drawer.
"String . . . you can begin screwing hooks into the ceiling while I look for paper bags." Returning several minutes later with a load of grocery bags, she reminded him
that Bhanjan Singh was still sitting under the tree in the
same position. "Should we nudge him? How long can
he sit like that?"

"No need to worry about him, he does it for hours,"
Alfie reassured her. "Look, I've run out of hooks, what
do I do now?"

Sister Hyacinthe showed him how to tie together
bunches of mustard, insert them into the paper bag and
suspend each one from a hook in the ceiling. They had

hung up three when a door slammed and Brill hailed them from the hallway. "Hey, come on," he shouted, "things are happening. I drove back to get you."

"They're free?" cried Sister Hyacinthe dropping scissors and string.

"Not yet. Hop into the van; Bhanjan Singh will look after Sister Ursula."

Bhanjan Singh was standing on the porch, vertical at last. "Trust me," he said gravely. "The Arab horse speeds fast, the camel plods slowly but it goes by day and night."

Sister Hyacinthe assumed this to mean that he was prepared to sacrifice non-violence for their cause, picked up her skirts, thanked him and climbed into the van beside Brill and Alfie. "I don't understand," she protested as the van turned and raced down the driveway to Fallen Stump Road.

"A picture is worth a thousand words," Brill told her, grinning. "It's been a busy morning and it's only just past noon. Its being a Saturday helped. That, and the fact that Sister John seems to have shared a cell last night with a remarkable young woman named Isabelle Irwin who was released at six this morning."

"He's being deliberately mysterious," Alfie told Sister Hyacinthe. "When he's like this there's absolutely nothing you can do. Hey, we're almost there, that's the court house up ahead."

Sister Hyacinthe glanced up Main Street and turned pale. "There's been an accident!" she gasped, clutching Alfie.

"No accident," Brill said firmly, and inserted the van into one of the last remaining parking spaces three blocks from the court house. "We have to walk now."

It was obvious why they had to walk the rest of the way: swarms of people surrounded the court house and overflowed into the street, which made traffic difficult on a busy Saturday afternoon and added more congestion and more people to the crowds. Signs on long sticks were being brandished; horns blew; men shouted, among them Hubie Johnson attempting to clear the street for cars, and all of this appeared to focus upon the steps of the court house. With uncanny skill Brill slipped through the crowd, pulling Sister Hyacinthe and Alfie behind him, and found a clear space just under the feet of General Grant.

Sister Hyacinthe stared at the tableau in front of her in astonishment. Praying conspicuously on the steps, and in full raiment, was Father Daniel O'Malley from the church around the corner: he had been kneeling there for two hours on a pneumatic pillow. Distributed up and down the stairs, but very carefully so not to obscure Father O'Malley, stood Sister Isabelle's contingent from Community House, a respectable and conservative group of priests and nuns carrying signs that read JESUS PICKED BEANS TOO. IS GATESVILLE GODLESS? LOVE THY NEIGHBOR DON'T JAIL HIM.

At the bottom of the steps Sister Isabelle had placed her group from the House of Hope, slightly less washed, younger and considerably more militant. Their placards read UP SHERIFF MCGEE, GATESVILLE OR BERCHTESGADEN? and IF THEY'RE GOOD ENOUGH TO PICK YOUR BEANS THEY'RE GOOD ENOUGH TO WALK YOUR STREETS.

Facing them in the opposite corner stood a small shabby cluster of migrant workers led by an exalted Melida who carried a sign WE'RE HUMAN TOO.

To Brill, who had been supervising and observing this phenomenon for several hours, it was all very readable, one of the more modest protests in which he had involved himself but nearly perfect in its spontaneity and indignation. As if on cue he watched the Baptist minister enter from right stage and stride up the stairs to join Father O'Malley on his knees. A few moments of silent prayer and the two men rose in time to greet Rabbi Schwartz, and as they gravely conferred together on the steps the Episcopalian minister rushed breathlessly up to join them, a little late because he had been golfing. A flashbulb exploded on the far left: the photographer from the Gatesville *Courier* had arrived, and Brill hazarded the guess that the mayor would follow on his heels.

Actually a popcorn vendor arrived first, but only a minute before the mayor's car made its way down the street and Hubie Johnson ordered the crowds to one side. Looking appropriately harassed and concerned, the mayor hurried up the stairs and vanished into the court house.

"It's going very well," said Alfie, busy explaining the rituals of protest to Sister Hyacinthe.

"It's thrilling," she said, her eyes shining.

The climax held within it all the grandness of a summit conference; after fifteen minutes a janitor came out to set up a microphone on the portico, and after perhaps half an hour—perfectly timed because the popcorn vendor had run out of popcorn—the two doors of the court house slowly opened and the four pastors filed out, looking pleased. The janitor followed carrying four chairs, and then returned with four more chairs, and the pastors seated themselves, their faces turned toward the door. Out of the shadows emerged Uncle Joe, propped up by a beaming mayor who led him, terrified, to a chair. A radiant Sister John followed, and then Naomi, looking amused. The crowd cheered wildly although Brill doubted if many knew what or whom they were cheering. The mayor, smiling broadly, stepped forward to the microphone and beckoned Sister John to stand at his side. Of Sheriff McGee there was no sign.

The mayor began to speak, but since he was running for reelection in the fall the point of his message was delayed by frequent references to Gatesville's sense of fair play, its generosity and its warm and neighborly heart with—as garnish—a number of references to himself for keeping the town up to snuff. Eventually, if unctuously, he came to the point: there had been an unhappy misunderstanding here in Gatesville, innocent people had been victimized but justice had now been done and Sister John, Miss Witkowski and Mr. Stout were being released from jail. Apologies had been extended and accepted, and the three bore the town no ill will.

"And I'd like to go on record as saying right here and now," he concluded, "that Gatesville is delighted to see the migrant workers in Gatesville at any time. In our churches . . . in our stores . . . on our streets."

Sister John received the mayor's words as a sign clearly sent to her from heaven. He did not mean a word of it, and after only five days out of cloister Sister John knew that he did not mean a word of it, but he had spoken the words publicly and she had no intention of allowing him to forget them. "We are happy to be free again," she said, handed the microphone for a response. "We are equally delighted," she added, smiling at the mayor, "to learn that migrant workers will always, in the future, be welcome in Gatesville. In your churches . . . in your stores . . . on your streets. Thank you, Mr. Mayor," she said, and stepped back from the microphone.

At this point Sister Isabelle signaled her groups to surge up the steps and surround the actors in the drama. It was a perfect denouement, the dropping of a curtain at a crucial punch line. Within minutes the sidewalks emptied and the shoppers returned to the stores, confident that God had somehow been served, for certainly with such a quota of priests, nuns and ministers in view something religious had to have happened in Gatesville today.

13

"Easy does it, Uncle Joe," said Brill, lifting him out of the van. "Left leg over the—that's it, now the other foot."

Uncle Joe's feet met solid earth and he straightened up. "Well now," he said in a quavering voice. "Well now . . ." Straightening brought him face to face with Brill and he looked startled. "This is a day the Lord made, young man. Where are we, Melida?"

"Back at Mr. Eaton's farm, Uncle Joe."

"Praise the Lord," he said, and with a nod at Sister John grasped his cane and took a step forward. Slowly, with Melida and Alice on either side, he maneuvered down the narrow lane toward a row of cabins under the trees. Beyond, as far as the eye could see, stretched acres of green in the sun, brightened by the colorful shirts and kerchiefs of workers on their knees.

They turned and climbed back into the van. "I don't think I've told you how beautiful you all look after a night in jail," Sister John said happily. "Who's guarding Sister Ursula?"

"Bhanjan Singh," said Brill, and turning the van around headed them back toward Fallen Stump Road.

"I worried terribly about you," confessed Sister Hyacinthe from the rear.

Sister John turned and gave her a warm smile. "I thought you might but it was quite unnecessary, you know. The hamburgers they sent in were greasy and it's true I didn't sleep a wink last night, but neither had anything to do with being ill-treated. How clever you and Sister Isabelle were," she told Brill. "I had no idea that's how things get done these days."

"It was nothing," Brill said modestly. "A little black-mail, a touch of chicanery, a few nudges . . ." He turned at their mailbox and drove up past the newly scythed lawn toward the house. "There they are," he said, point-ing. "Sitting on chairs in the sun. Wonder how Bhanjan Singh managed *that*."

As the van drew to a stop beside the front porch Bhanjan Singh rose, his round face beaming with plea-sure. " 'Evening precedes morning and night becomes dawn,' " he said, and moving forward to meet Sister John, he pressed both of her hands in his. "I am so glad to see you safely back. Here also is the letter that ar-rived for you yesterday. Sister Hyacinthe forgot to take it to you when she left."

"Thank you, Bhanjan Singh," she said with a glance at the postmark.

Sister Ursula remained in his chair but his face, had brightened and he waved a hand. "It's a damn lucky day for you," he told her. "How did you like jail?"

"It radicalized me," she told him. "I'm not sure what the word means but it has an electric sound and I feel electrified."

"AC or DC?" quipped Alfie.

"We'll join you," said Sister John, dropping to the ground and arranging her skirts around her. "What are we interrupting?"

"A celebration of the senses," Sister Ursula told her gloomily. "The sun is the giver of life, he says, and he's also been lecturing me on matter, energy, mass and illusion. Did you know that no problems really exist in the world and that I'm only a prisoner of my thoughts?"

"Exactly what I've been telling you," Sister John said unfeelingly, and peeled back the flap of her letter.

"You haven't had any sleep, don't you want to rest first?" Sister Hyacinthe asked her curiously.

"With so much to be done? Nonsense I'll have a cup of tea later instead. Right now I want to read this; it's from the abbess." Opening the letter she scanned it and nodded. "Yes, this is what I wanted to know, I'll read it aloud. Where are you going, Sister Ursula?"

"You may not be sleepy but I am," he said. "I can hardly keep my eyes open."

Watching him leave, Bhanjan said with a sigh, "He that will eat the kernel must first crack the nut. . . . I fear I was too abstract; it is always so difficult to talk to beginners."

"Or to people with closed minds," said Alfie. "Read the letter, Sister John."

"I will," she said, and leaned over it. "First of all the abbess stresses that this information is privileged, and the official records are in Switzerland and so on and so on, but I'll read the important section. She's replying about Sister Emma and she writes: 'I do remember Mother Clothilde saying that at seventeen Sister Emma found herself caring deeply for an older man, a close friend of her family. There was an engagement, a wedding date was set, but a few weeks before the wedding Sister Emma's call to God proved the stronger: she broke off the engagement and entered a nearby convent as novitiate.

" 'When she came to us some months later—do you remember how sweet and grave and dedicated she was?—the man who loved her tried many times to see her. About him I know nothing,' " continued Sister John, reading, " 'except that Mother Clothilde saw him in her office a number of times, always late at night and secretly. She confided in me, I think, because these were such exhausting interviews, and very troubling to her, for she said the man was alternately stormy, heart-broken, threatening and bitter at losing Sister Emma to God. (How frail human beings can be!) I remember that Mother Clothilde prayed long and hard for the man, and asked me to do the same.

" 'All this I thought I'd forgotten—it seems so many years ago—but your query has brought it back to me. Other than this Mother Clothilde's files tell me only that Sister Emma was born in Roslyn, Long Island, on June 30, 1933, under the name of Linda Elizabeth Scozzafava, and that she was, as you know, a person of great gentleness and sweetness, may God rest her soul.' "

"Scozzafava," said Sister Hyacinthe, frowning.

"Yes, Scozzafava," repeated Sister John, and put down the letter, nodding. "Things begin to fit. It was Mr. Moretti, of course, to whom Sister Emma was engaged to be married."

"But where have I heard the name Scozzafava before?" asked Alfie.

"Exactly," said Sister John. "Sheriff McGee mentioned it to us the first evening he came here, he thought the house belonged to a Frank Scozzafava." She added thoughtfully, "And I think we must pray very very hard."

"Why?" asked Sister Hyacinthe.

She glanced at Bhanjan Singh and smiled faintly. "Because to tread with impunity upon a tiger's tail, breathless caution is required. I think," she said, "it's time we have a very serious talk. Preferably over a cup of peppermint tea. Shall we go, inside? You see," she added, brushing the grass from her skirts. "I accomplished some very useful thinking in jail, after Sister Isabelle was released, and I reached several conclusions, all of them rather dismaying."

"Dangerous?" asked Alfie hopefully.

"Oh, I hope not," she said, "but there may not be much time left to *arrange* things."

Once inside she paused and stood looking into the living room as if she'd forgotten what it looked like, then nodded and continued on through the passage to the kitchen. Here she abruptly stopped. "Good heavens, what's been happening here?"

"Oh, that," said Alfie proudly, "Sister Hyacinthe and I were hanging up mustard to dry."

"No, no, not that," said Sister John, brushing this aside impatiently. "All of Sister Hyacinthe's rooms look like greenhouses eventually. I mean the pantry."

At first no one understood what she meant because the pantry looked an oasis of order compared to the kitchen. The late afternoon sun poured through its window, illuminating the wide floor boards, here and there touching a white crock on the shelves and glancing off two loaves of foil-wrapped abbey bread. Then Alfie re-

membered that the sun ought not to be flooding the pantry because he had boarded up the window. He cried,
"Good God, we've been burgled!"

"But this is not possible," protested Bhanjan Singh.
"Sister Ursula and I have been here all afternoon."

"But outside on the front lawn," pointed out Naomi.

"What's missing?" asked Brill.

Sister John walked into the pantry, glanced at the
higher shelf and said dryly, "Three containers of sugar."

"I don't understand," complained Sister Hyacinthe.
"Who could have stolen them in broad daylight? Who
would have dared pry loose the boards and crawl
through the window?"

"Someone who badly wanted those three jars," said
Brill grimly. "Someone who knew that we'd be downtown seeing Sister John and Naomi released, leaving
only two of us behind, and someone who knew—or
thought—there was cocaine here."

"But it isn't," pointed out Sister Hyacinthe.

"No, it isn't but our burglar didn't know that. There's
only one person I can think of who fills that bill, or else
this house is under continuous surveillance, or—" He
leaned over and picked up a small dark object lying on
the floor under the window. "This wasn't in the pantry
before was it?" he asked. "I think our burglar left a calling card." He handed Sister John a long fat cigar.

"Sani-Smoke." she said, reading the gold print on the
black label. "Made in Zambia, Central Africa. Good
heavens the *sheriff* broke into our pantry?"

"I don't know who else," Brill said. "He was conspicuously absent from the court house steps this afternoon, he'd know by now—he must—that it was cocaine

he took away with him on Thursday and he knows where he found it."

Sister Hyacinthe, examining the cigar, said dryly, "He must have been carrying it in his back hip pocket again."

"But a sheriff?" protested Sister John. "The world is falling apart around us and no one screams? A man with his job and reputation? Why would he have done such a thing?"

Alfie said cheerfully, "Overtaken by a spasm of pernicious greed, I imagine. Selling fifteen pounds of snow on the open market would net him a fortune bigger than his reputation, which isn't all that great anyway, you know."

Bhanjan Singh said softly, " 'To an ass a thistle is a delicious fruit. The ass eats the thistle. He remains an ass.' "

"Of course he's an ass but what do we *do*?" asked Sister Hyacinthe.

Sister John turned away, her face troubled. "What we must do is make plans," she said, "because if it was the sheriff in our pantry—" Removing a pile of mustard from the chair, she dropped it to the floor and sat down at the kitchen table. "I think it's time to tell you what Sister Hyacinthe and I discovered in the well on the day we arrived. I don't know how much time we have left us, and Sister Hyacinthe and I need your help."

"But it isn't our secret to tell!" gasped Sister Hyacinthe.

"You don't feel they can be trusted?" asked Sister John, suddenly grave.

"Of course they can be trusted but—"

"I think they can be trusted, too," said Sister John,

nodding. "We haven't even finished counting it yet but I know that on Monday morning it simply has to be placed in a safe-deposit box, and under no circumstances will I step out of this house without a convoy of people guarding it."

"Guarding what?" asked Naomi, distributing chunks of goats' cheese.

"Money. An incredible amount of it, with a great deal more to be counted."

"Good God, I missed that too?" gasped Alfie.

"Well, you can't have everything," Sister Hyacinthe told him indignantly. "You found the bug and the secret passage, you can't begrudge us the money and Sister Ursula."

"It was hidden in the well," pointed out Sister John, as if this explained everything, "and its being there changes all the recommendations I plan to make to the abbess for the use of the property."

"You're not going to sell?" Brill sounded startled.

"I expect you'll want to turn it into a retreat," put in Naomi. "Everyone does."

"No," said Sister John, rising, "no, I don't have a retreat in mind at all." She glanced at her watch. "It's growing late—nearly five o'clock—and I was going to ask you to help us finish counting the money. It's hidden in the basement."

"You're being mysterious," pointed out Naomi, following her to the cellar door. "Wells ... money ... your plans for it. Aren't you going to tell us what you have in mind for the property?"

"Later," said Sister John, starting down the stairs. "It all depends on how much money there is. So far I've counted up to ninety-nine thousand," she said, and ignoring their shocked gasps she added casually, "What I'm hoping for is half a million. . . ."

In the end neither the pickle barrel nor the Steinway yielded up half a million but the total counting proved to be four hundred twenty-one thousand and nine dollars and was enough, said Alfie, to give him indigestion for months.

"Like an orgy," said Sister Hyacinthe knowingly.

"Well, not quite," Alfie told her reproachfully, "but it's an awful lot of paper. It's taken us nearly three hours, it's past seven o'clock and I'm famished."

"And all this was down a *well*?" echoed Naomi.

"Yes, in a genuine cowhide suitcase with a 1963 New York *Daily News* tucked inside."

Brill glanced at her curiously as he wrote down the final tally. "You've had all this lying around here for six days and you haven't felt the least uneasy?"

"Nothing," said Sister John, "could happen to the money if it's intended for us, and I'm sure it must be because God has been guiding us with a very firm hand."

"Even to jail?" asked Naomi.

"But of course," said Sister John impatiently. "That was one of the most important experiences of my life. You mustn't feel that good comes only from happy things, you know, it's often the most painful experiences that bring enlightenment."

"Now you sound just like Bhanjan Singh," Brill told her, amused.

Here Naomi returned carrying paper grocery bags and rubber bands and they went to work again binding up the bills and stowing them neatly away for the trip on Monday to the safe-deposit box. This done, they per-

suaded Sister John to move the bags to a safer place
now that Sister Ursula had discovered the preserve
closet to be a direct route to the wine cellar.

"Where, then?" asked Sister John as they labored upstairs with the bags and deposited them on the kitchen
floor. "We have bags of this and bags of that; if we're
not careful we'll end up putting mustard in the safe-
deposit box."

"I say the second floor because that's where you
sleep," said Brill. "In case of fire you just toss the bags
out the window. Yourselves, too," he added generously.

"Too close to Sister Ursula; that man has a definite
nose for money," said Alfie.

"What about the refrigerator?" asked Sister Hyacinthe. "It's empty nearly all the time."

This appeared logical to them and they carried the
paper bags of money to the refrigerator and stowed
them away inside, which reminded Alfie that it was
long past his dinner hour. When he ventured to speak of
this Naomi gave him a quelling glance. "You've forgotten. Sister John promised to tell us when the money was
counted what she hopes to do with this incredible four
hundred thousand."

"Four hundred twenty-one thousand and nine," corrected Sister Hyacinthe.

"To be used for the glory of God," said Sister John,
her eyes luminous. "I'd be delighted to tell you because
if it weren't for you—I felt it all take shape in the early
hours of the morning, after Sister Isabelle was bailed
out of jail. I *saw* it." She walked to the door and looked
out over the garden through the privet hedge to the line
of woods beyond. "I saw it very clearly," she said, her
voice dreaming. "A small community, perhaps thirty

migrant families with their children. . . . I saw thirty small houses with room for little gardens behind them, and one large communal garden—perhaps seventy-five acres—where a number of cash crops could be raised for the support of all the families. The remaining acres would be woods. I saw the men going off to pick beans and grapes and apples for neighboring farmers but it would be done by contract, as free men, and they'd come home at night to their own homes. I saw the shacks no longer used and collapsing, the children growing educated, the women growing a crop very new to them—hope." She turned and said almost defiantly. "They've done something like that in Florida, Sister Isabelle told me so. Thirty families wouldn't be *many*, but if you toss just one pebble into a pond the ripples reach the farthest shore."

There was a long silence and then Naomi said skeptically. "In *Gatesville*?"

Brill said nothing; his hands hung at his sides, his eyes remote while he thought about it. At last he said curtly, "Do you know—can you possibly realize—what you'd be up against? City zoning laws, sewage commissions, roads, taxes, bureaucratic snarls, indifferent contractors, inflated costs, not to mention prejudice, and everyone thinking it wonderful but wanting it built somewhere else?"

Sister John said in a shocked voice, "Of course it wouldn't be *easy*."

"You're going to recommend that to the abbess?" faltered Sister Hyacinthe. "But who would do all that work?"

Alfie gave her an amused glance. "Sister John, of course."

"But she's in cloister!"

Bhanjan Singh chuckled. "If in cloister she has grown the inner strength of ten would you have her spend it on mending a printing press when she could mend a little of the world? As your Ecclesiastes says, to everything there is a season ... or if I may quote the I Ching, 'Respectfully contemplate the ebb and flow, the unending succession of repletion and depletion that constitutes the way to heaven.'"

"Well?" said Alfie, staring at Brill.

A slow smile spread across Brill's bearded face. "It's great, it's really beautiful. Maybe I'm jealous, being a burned-out case at twenty-five, tired of hassles, cynical and ready for my own kind of cloister. But, I've got some glorious leftover ideas I can bequeath you, Sister John, I can give you hard-earned tips on cost sheets, stubborn mayors, the media and hostile zoning boards."

"I know that," Sister John said simply. "Can we begin talking about it right now?"

"There goes dinner," sighed Alfie, and then, brightening, "I'll tell you what. Yesterday was payday. You and Brill talk and I'll drive to that fried chicken place down the road and buy everybody a rousing good dinner. My treat."

"I'll pay for ice cream," volunteered Naomi.

"A feast," marveled Sister Hyacinthe. "Won't Sister Ursula be pleased? I'll just run up and tell him."

"Ask him what flavor ice cream," Naomi called after her, and they moved slowly into the hall, Brill and Naomi counting money into Alfie's palm.

Sister Hyacinthe hurried eagerly back down the stairs, and from the landing Sister Ursula called, "Make mine any exotic flavor they have, I'm very partial to things like pistachio nut and almond chip."

Alfie grinned. "I would have guessed that even if you hadn't told me, Sister Ursula." He stood in the doorway shrugging into a sweater and then he leaned forward, peering intently through the screen door as he wrestled with its sleeves. "Who the heck's sitting in Mr. Armisbruck's van?"

"No one, of course," said Sister John, coming to his side and glancing down the steps toward the car. "That's strange," she added, seeing the silhouette of a figure seated at the wheel.

"What's strange?" asked Brill.

Without replying Sister John opened the door and walked across to the porch and down the steps; Brill and Alfie followed. "Hey, wait for me," Naomi called. "I'm supposed to carry the ice cream, remember?"

Sister John walked around the front of the van, glancing through the windshield as she approached the door beside the driver's seat. She said in a quiet voice, "It's Sheriff McGee," and her right hand moved to describe the sign of a cross.

For a moment Alfie didn't understand. He said, "Hey, Sheriff!" and reaching in front of Sister John wrenched open the door of the van.

The sheriff, sitting rigidly upright, fell across the wheel with his face turned toward them. It was obvious from his wide and vacant stare that he was dead: there was a wet red bullet hole between his eyes.

"Oboy," said Alfie, swallowing with difficulty.

"What is it?" asked Sister Hyacinthe, coming up behind him.

"Sheriff McGee—he's dead."

"That's ridiculous," said Sister Hyacinthe. "How can he be dead when only a few hours ago he stole our sugar?"

"I don't know, Sister Hyacinthe, he's dead, that's all. Somebody shot him."

"You're absolutely sure he's *dead*?" said Brill, looking dazed.

"Absolutely," Alfie said, drawing back and looking a little sick. "There's an even bigger hole in the back of his head and no sign of any heartbeat." He stood staring at the sheriff, and when he looked up, his gaze moving to the driveway, the last vestige of color drained from his face. "Good God, somebody's coming," he said in an anguished voice. "A car with lots of men in it."

"Oh dear," said Sister John, "I certainly didn't expect them so soon."

14

"Expect who?" demanded Sister Hyacinthe.

"Never mind who—hide the sheriff," cried Alfie. "Good God, how could we ever explain him? Hide him in the back."

"No time," said Brill. "Push him down."

Sister John closed her eyes, folded her hands and murmured, "Graciously hear, O Lord, the prayers we address to Thee, by which we humbly entreat Thy mercy—"

"He won't stay down, he keeps popping up. Brill, for heaven's sake help me!"

"—to receive into the kingdom of peace and light the soul of Thy servant Sheriff McGee—"

"He's down, thank God. Close the door on him, Naomi."

"They're here," said Brill. "Sister John?"

"Amen," she finished, and opened her eyes.

A long blue limousine came to a stop at a discreet distance from the van, a car door flew open and two men jumped out, one racing to the east corner of the house and vanishing into the shrubbery, the other hurry-

ing to the west side. Neither gave so much as a glance
to the small group clustered around the van. The driver
of the car stepped out, opened the right-hand rear door
and helped a man in a dark pin-stripe suit to descend.
He was short and silverhaired, impeccably groomed
with a face that bore slashing black lines like a Buffet
print: a pair of sharp verticals from nose to mouth, a
pair of thick horizontal brows, a deep vertical between
the eyes. "All right," he said, looking them over coldly,
"no need to be frightened, nobody's going to get hurt,
this is only a social call. Just move away from that van
now—"

"Gladly," gasped Alfie.

"—and go back in the house."

"Sister John, who *are* these men?" Sister Hyacinthe
asked plaintively.

"I think," she said, "that we are being visited by the
Mafia."

"You're kidding," said Alfie.

"You've got to be kidding," said Naomi.

"Mafia?" repeated Brill, and then with dawning comprehension, *"Mafia?"*

"And I believe," added Sister John with a pleasant
smile, "that this would be Mr. Scozzafava—Mr. Frank
Scozzafava—am I right?"

Instead of responding, the man looked appalled. "Get
them inside," he ordered sharply. "Hide the car in the
barn. Pronto."

"It's the Mafia all right," said Naomi.

"And if we don't want to go?" asked Alfie.

"Don't be funny," snapped the man. "I told you this
is a social call—see you keep it that way." He turned on
his heel and stalked up the steps to the porch, waved

Bhanjan Singh aside from the door and went into the house.

"Social call?" protested Alfie. "One of those first two men carried a gun, I swear it."

"Then he has very poor manners," said Sister John, and lifting her skirts led the way up the porch steps. Finding Bhanjan Singh just inside the door, she said in a low voice, "Sister Ursula?"

He lifted his eyes heavenward, she nodded and walked into the living room where their newest guest stood scowling. "All right, how do you know who I am?" he demanded.

"You really are Mr. Scozzafava then," said Sister John pleased. "Would you be Sister Emma's father, or perhaps a brother?"

He stopped in the act of lighting a cigarette with a dazzling gold lighter. "So that's it, you're from St. Tabitha's Abbey. But my daughter's dead," he pointed out, "and what's more to the point she'd be alive now if she'd listened to her father's advice and married instead, so we'll change the subject because I didn't come here to talk about my daughter."

"I didn't think you had," Sister John told him, "but you did say this is purely a social call?"

"I never say what I don't mean." He observed her frankly, with irony in his gaze. "You're a tough cookie, Sister, you don't scare easy, you've given us a hard time not budging from this house." He glanced toward the hall and casually waved a hand. "You others stay out there, I'll deal directly with the sister here. Sit down, Sister."

Sister John seated herself on the couch and told him reassuringly, "You needn't reproach yourself, Mr.

Scozzafava, you certainly did all you could to encourage us to leave, in fact some of your efforts were very ingenious, but obviously God didn't want us to go."

"Please, spare me a sermon," he told her, holding up a hand. "I'd rather keep the house, frankly; it's been useful, but if Joe left it to you legally I'll throw in the towel like a gentleman. However, there happen to be some things here that belong to us," he added, fixing her with a chilly eye, "and we've come to move them out. We can, I think, be reasonable about this?"

"Probably," said Sister John, and asked with interest, "What would those things be?"

"Nothing either you or your abbey could possibly be interested in. Boys—you know where to look, get moving. Where's Joe?"

"Here, boss," said a fourth man, strolling in through the front door. "The car's in the barn, the place checked back and front and Roy's going to guard the front door."

As the light in the hall illuminated the man's face Sister Hyacinthe gasped, "Why, Mr. Ianicelli!"

He gave her a sheepish glance and tipped his hat. "Evening, Sister."

"And Mr. Smith from the Cowbell Dairy!" exclaimed Sister John, her gaze moving to the man behind him. "Is Mr. Giovianni here, too?"

Ianicelli looked blank. "Giovianni? Don't know any Giovianni."

"Perhaps he really was a census taker then," she said, "I don't believe you've met my companions, Mr. Scozzafava. That's Sister Hyacinthe in the doorway, and behind her is Mr. Bhanjan Singh, and next to him is—"

Mr. Scozzafava's hand moved again to cut her off.

"Please, Sister, we'll be out of here in five minutes. Okay, Joe, Charlie, Pete, get moving, let's wrap this up."

They moved in unison out of the hall and disappeared into the kitchen. In the ensuing void Alfie inched his way into the living room and perched on the edge of a chair, earning him a hard glance from Mr. Scozzafava but no comment. The others simply stood and looked at Mr. Scozzafava curiously, as if a rare bird of prey had landed by chance in their living room. The wait was brief; Charlie came back and said bluntly, "It's not there, boss."

Scozzafava's black brows lifted. "Then search the house, Charlie, search it from attic to cellar. And hurry it up," he added with a glance at his watch.

Sister John received news of a search without visible alarm but her thoughts went at once to the refrigerator, where $421,009 rested on the shelves in brown grocery bags; it suddenly seemed a most reckless hiding place. Her mind raced ahead, envisioning its discovery, searching for a solution, and fell at last upon an idea dazzling in its simplicity. She said politely to Mr. Scozzafava, "If your searching is going to take a while I do wonder if you'd mind our going on with the work we were doing? We're drying herbs in the kitchen."

"Drying *what*?" His brows flew up again.

"Mustard," she told him. "The yellow wild flowers Alfie scythed this morning, or didn't you," she asked, "realize that mustard is made from mustard plants?"

"Is it?" Scozzafava said indifferently, and then with a shrug, "This room is boring. Show me."

"Of course," she said, rising, and catching Alfie's eye remarked casually, "Do you remember, Alfie, where I was afraid the mustard might *accidentally be placed on Monday morning*? The paper bags ought to be hung up now."

Alfie, suddenly alert, said, "Oh," and then *"Oh!"* and sprang to his feet.

Mr. Scozzafava followed them into the kitchen and was shown the piles of mustard on the table—indeed it was difficult to ignore them—and Sister Hyacinthe was persuaded to demonstrate how the stalks were tied together and inserted into bags. Just to make certain that Mr. Scozzafava understood the entire process Sister John stood on a chair and removed one of the three bags hanging from the ceiling, opened it and showed him its contents.

"Yes, yes, never mind," he said impatiently. "I get the idea."

"Good," said Sister John, poured him a cup of luke-warm tea and placed him in a chair with his back to the refrigerator. Brill climbed on a chair. Alfie took a position next to the refrigerator, quietly opened the door and began handing out bags of money to Naomi, who knotted string around them, so that while Sister Hyacinthe continued tying her bouquets of fragrant mustard, dropping them innocently to the floor, Brill suspended bags of money from the ceiling. It was, thought Alfie, an inspired piece of sleight of hand. While they worked, Mr. Scozzafava's men completed their search upstairs, fanned out through the living room and kitchen and then moved down to the cellar, Charlie peering into the refrigerator just before he joined the others. By this time, however, the last bag was knotted to a hook and the kitchen had a festive air, with dozens of balloon-like bags swinging idly from their strings. All that was needed, said Naomi, was birthday hats and favors.

"Found it!" came a triumphant shout from the cellar, and Mr. Scozzafava shouted back, "Good! Bring it upstairs and let's get out of here."

"Only thing is," said Charlie, walking into the kitchen, "three jars are missing. We're fifteen pounds short."

They waited while Mr. Scozzafava digested this fact. "Tiresome," he said, frowning. "I don't like to hear that, don't like it at all." He sat brooding over his teacup, eyes thoughtful, fingers tapping idly on the table. "All right," he said, reaching a decision, and directed a stern glance at Sister John. "What we're looking for was left on the top shelf in the pantry. Large glass jars labeled sugar."

"Oh, that," said Sister John.

"We're missing some of it."

She nodded. "Yes, you would be. Sheriff McGee took away some of it, of course, and then this afternoon—"

Mr. Scozzafava's eyes narrowed. "Who?"

"Sheriff McGee."

Scozzafava stared at her. "Sheriff McGee removed fifteen pounds?"

"Not at first," Sister John assured him. "He only took a little away on Thursday—spilling it very carelessly on the pantry floor, I might add. Then this afternoon three jars were taken while we were downtown."

"Taken?"

"It was a burglary," said Sister John, looking him straight in the eye. "Naturally it was a burglary since the pantry window had been boarded up and someone removed the boards and stole the sugar. We could only assume it was the sheriff because he left behind— Where is it, Brill?"

"Here on the table," Brill said, and reached over and handed the cigar to Mr. Scozzafava.

Scozzafava glanced at the label and his jaw tightened. "Charlie," he said in a dangerous voice, "find McGee. Anybody know where the hell McGee is at this hour?"

"Actually," said Sister John helpfully, "he's outside the house in Mr. Armisbruck's van."

"What the hell's he doing there?" asked Scozzafava.

"Someone shot him."

"Will somebody see what the hell she's talking about?" demanded Scozzafava. "For the love of God—no, no it's impossible."

Charlie shot out of the room jet-propelled; they waited in silence until he shot back into the room. "Boss, he's dead as a mackerel," he gasped. "It's true, boss, I shine my light in the front seat and McGee's lying there with a shot between his eyes. Geez, boss, the sister's right."

Scozzafava stared incredulously at Sister John. "All the time we've been sharing this friendly social call you knew there was a dead sheriff outside?"

"I assumed, of course, that *you* shot him," said Sister John.

"Me?" He looked astonished. "The guy's on my payroll and I should shoot him?"

"Ah," murmured Sister John, nodding.

"What's more he's a friend of mine."

"Was," pointed out Ianicelli, "and not so good a

friend if he stole fifteen pounds of you-know-what, boss."

"With the money I pay him?" said Scozzafava, shaking his head. "Christ, is nothing sacred? Last week Ev Brown, today Sheriff McGee—Okay, let's skip that for the moment. Let's start with the fact he's dead and take it slow and easy, boys. For instance if he's dead somebody had to kill him. The question is, who?"

"One of this bunch, boss?"

Scozzafava's glance moved over Alfie, Brill, Naomi, Bhanjan Singh and dismissed them contemptuously. "Amateurs," he said. "Let me think a minute." Again there was silence, interrupted only by Scozzafava's fingers impatiently tapping the table. He suddenly snapped his fingers and pointed at Sister John. "You," he said. "You mentioned a Giovianni." When she nodded he said, "Charlie, what's the name of that pretty guy with teeth who works for Grassia? Used to be Nick's bag man."

"Giovianni, boss."

Scozzafava nodded. "I'm beginning to smell something, Joe, something's getting through to me. Joe, I want you should call Grassia. Tell him I want a sitdown. Tell him where we are—I have a feeling when he hears where we are it'll be enough to bring him running. Tell him we've got to talk."

"Boss, you think—"

"Never mind what I think, find a telephone and call him. He should be in Scarsdale, it's Saturday night and he's a family man. Tell him I got four men with me and he can bring four. Tell him it's urgent."

"Right, boss," he said, and hurried out of the room.

Mr. Scozzafava stood up slowly and looked around

the room like a man suddenly released from an unsatisfying and constricting role. "This is no longer a social call," he announced flatly. "Charlie, move these people into the living room and then take over the back door here. Roy, you find a shovel and start digging outside, some nice quiet corner in the garden, you understand? One can't be too careful."

"I understand, boss," Roy said, and grinned unpleasantly at Sister John as he strode past her.

15

"I don't like the odds," murmured Alfie as they were herded into the living room. "I get the distinct impression that Mr. Scozzafava isn't planning to plant nasturtiums in that hole in the back yard."

"No," said Naomi distastefully. *"Us."*

It had grown dark outside while they were in the kitchen, and the clock on the mantel said half-past nine. Turning on the light Brill said, "There are six of us against their five, you know."

Alfie snorted. "I can kick, Naomi knows how to bite, and you won a Golden Gloves championship, but I can't see Sister Hyacinthe, Bhanjan Singh and Sister John brawling, can you?"

"No, indeed," said Bhanjan Singh, seating himself on the floor and tucking his legs under him. "Wisdom goes beyond strength."

"I agree wholeheartedly," said Sister John, and turning to Brill, said, "We were going to talk about plans for the migrant village, you know. There's a map of the property on the mantel." She walked resolutely to the mantel, head high, and returned to the couch. "I've been wondering, would it save money to place the houses in a row, with one furnace for every two or three houses, and the basements connecting, or would it be more sensible to have the houses detached?"

Looking a little dazed, Brill sat down beside her. "It depends, of course ... Where will your sewage lines enter?"

"Isn't she worried?" Naomi asked Sister Hyacinthe.

"Oh, I don't think so. She has perfect faith, you know."

"Maddening," said Naomi, and turned fiercely to Bhanjan Singh. "Faith in what, Bhanjan? *Is* there a God?"

With his eyes closed Bhanjan Singh said serenely, "Man has taken huge steps forward and has proven that God cannot exist. He sees only the steps behind him; what he does not see are the steps remaining ahead. He rests, believing he knows all."

"Isn't there something we can do?" demanded Alfie. "Good God, when this Grassia comes he'll bring *more* men."

"Maybe they'll have a fight and kill each other off and we can plant *them* in the garden," said Naomi.

Bhanjan Singh opened his eyes. "All wisdom can be stated in two lines: what is done for you—allow it to be done. What you must do for yourself—make sure you do it."

"What you must do for yourself ..." echoed Brill, suddenly thoughtful. He looked entranced, and then gleeful, and reached over Sister John's lap to grasp her notebook. "Tear off a corner of your paper for me, will you?" he asked.

"Whatever for?"

"Never mind, there's a wild chance if I do this right." He nibbled the tip of his pencil, hesitated a moment and then began scribbling. "Think you could get this into the bag of garbage under the kitchen sink? It's important."

"Just—throw it away?" faltered Sister John, and when he nodded she said, "How very odd. I'll try, of course."

Leaving the couch, she headed for the kitchen. Mr. Scozzafava, reading a *Daily News* in the dining room, glanced up without interest and she successfully negotiated the passage into the kitchen, glancing at Brill's note as she went. On it he had scribbled: JOHN! SATURDAY NIGHT JULY 11, 12 MIDNIGHT MEETING, BLACK LIBERATION ARMY AND WEATHERMEN. BE ABSOLUTELY SURE YOU'RE NOT FOLLOWED. YOU KNOW WHERE I AM, NUNS ARE OKAY. BRILL.

She walked into the kitchen and deposited the note in the bag of garbage, empty of all but two of Alfie's Coke tins and a few snips of string. Charlie, seated on a stool by the back door, watched her moodily.

"What a mess," said Brill, following her out into the kitchen. He began plucking stalks of mustard from the floor and stuffing them into the garbage. "Anything else to go? I'll take it out to the pail."

At this Charlie slid off the stool, saying threateningly, "Oh no you won't."

"The sister wants the garbage out," Brill told him coldly. "You see any reason why the garbage can't go out?"

"None at all but *you're* not taking it out, brother. Get lost, I'll take it. Where's it go?"

"The bucket's at the bottom of the porch steps."

Charlie nodded, took the bag and carried it out, leaving Brill with a scowl on his face. "There's a man who's probably going to execute me before dawn ... Well, anyway, that's done. I have, you might say, shot an arrow into the air, to fall to earth I know not where. What shall we do next now?"

"Wait," said Sister John confidently, "and pray."

It was eleven o'clock when Mr. Ianicelli returned, walking into the hall and banging the screen door behind him. Glancing into the dining room he said, "Grassia's here, boss, we stashed the cars in the barn."

Scozzafava put down his newspaper. "What took you so long?"

"He wasn't at his house, he was at some damn fool church reception."

The screen door whined again and a burly man walked in wearing a light cashmere coat against the chills of the night. His face was large, with blunt, curiously flat features. He stopped in the hall, blinking at the bright lights, and then glanced into the living room. If he was surprised to find it occupied by six people, two of them nuns, he gave no evidence of it. He nodded to them pleasantly and turned toward the dining room. "Christ, Frank," he said, unbelting his coat, "I certainly am surprised to see you here. You been using this place, too?"

Mr. Giovianni followed him inside, dressed tonight in a white suit and plaid tie, but the three men behind him still wore the belted raincoats they had worn in the garden on Monday night.

Without preamble Scozzafava said, "Who shot McGee?"

"Fred," said Grassia, taking a chair opposite Scozzafava at the dining-room table. With a jerk of his head toward the living room he asked, "You care if they hear this?"

"It's too late for that," said Scozzafava with a shrug. "Why the hell did Fred shoot McGee?"

"Because," Grassia said, inserting a cigar between his lips and lighting it, "McGee had the gall to sell Fred fifteen pounds of cocaine that turned out to be sugar. Plain old table sugar." His voice was reproachful. "You know we can't stand for a double cross like that, Frank."

Scozzafava nodded. "It was my cocaine he stole, Nick, I'm missing exactly fifteen pounds."

"Yeah? He pull the double cross on you too, then? Fred figured it had to be your snow, seeing as how he's your man, but when he found it was sugar—"

"A rotten apple," Scozzafava said, nodding. "Okay, fair enough, no hard feelings, except what happened to the real stuff, the cocaine? It doesn't make sense, McGee pulling a stupid trick like that. The sisters here have proof McGee snatched the fifteen pounds out of the pantry just this afternoon."

Grassia's jaw dropped. "You had it here, Frank?" He stabbed his brow with the back of his hand. "If I'd only known! Christ, we been using the house, too, Frank. How the hell did these nuns get here, anyway? You could have knocked me over with a feather when the boys told me the place is suddenly occupied."

"Turns out to have been Joe Moretti's place legally, Nick. He died and left it to nuns."

"It still belonged to him!" Grassia shook his head in

wonder. "Those were the days, remember Frank? He was a good boss before he got deported and we all split. Beautiful man."

"We split but I don't know why you thought you could go on using the house, Nick, when it was me who took Joe's place."

Grassia shrugged. "We always used it when Moretti was boss, didn't we? He'd send me here as often as he did you, Frank. Habit, that's all." He sounded aggrieved. "Hell, we'd all been Moretti's men and then Picolo split and I went with him, and then Picolo went up the river and I took over; how was I to know you were using the place too?"

"I had the keys, you ever have the keys, Nick?"

"No, but—"

Scozzafava jerked his head toward the rear of the house. "Just the outside?"

"Okay, so why not?" asked Grassia, shrugging. "A few bodies here and there—it's nice and quiet, just like a cemetery. Which brings me to another point, Frank. One of my best men shot a guy here last weekend and loused up the job. My best hit man."

Scozzafava's glance was sympathetic. "Would that be Fingers Jacoby they found Wednesday in the Roslyn parking lot?"

Grassia nodded. "My best man, Frank. Broke my heart to put out a contract on him."

Scozzafava shook his head. "Even the best of them lose the silver touch, Nick, but I never would have believed it of Fingers Jacoby." He looked pensive. "You say he did it here, Nick?"

Grassia nodded. "Outside, in the back."

"And Fingers missed?"

"He missed all right," Grassia said grimly, knocking the ashes from his cigar. "We never found no body, not even a drop of blood."

He looked up, and seeing the expression on Scozzafava's face he froze with the cigar halfway to his lips. There was a long silence and then both men turned their faces to the living room, their eyes resting with interest on Sister John and Sister Hyacinthe. Scozzafava said softly, "Cocaine turns to sugar, and bodies disappear. . . . Charlie?" he shouted, and in an aside to Grassia explained, "Charlie's my hit man, the only man with a gun. You come armed, Nick?"

Nick looked affronted. "To a sit-down? I trusted you, Frank."

"Charlie," he said as Charlie came in from the kitchen, "take another look at the cocaine you brought up from the cellar. Taste it, smell it, make sure it's the real thing. Where'd you leave it, Charlie?"

"Right here on the stairs in the hall, boss."

"Okay, bring it here."

In the living room Sister John turned to the others and said in a low voice, "This is our chance, of course. I'll give them the real snow in exchange for your safety, it's the only thing to do."

"I hate to disillusion you," Alfie told her, "but I think it's rather late for that. We know too much, we know who killed Sheriff McGee and who killed someone called Fingers Jacoby, and—what's the matter with Charlie?" he asked, staring into the hall. "He looks as if he's seeing a ghost."

Charlie was staring openmouthed at a point in the curving staircase beyond their vision. He said, "It's gone, boss, the sugar's gone. We stashed it right here, halfway up the stairs out of the way—so help me we did—and it's gone."

With a martyred sigh Scozzafava rose and walked into the hall where he, too, stared, apparently at an empty staircase. "It didn't just walk off by itself," he pointed out testily. "Search the damn house again; there has to be somebody else here."

"Or the house could be haunted," put in Sister John quickly from the living room. "We had the most extraordinary experience the other night. Voices crying, chains rattling, a glowing face at the window . . ."

Scozzafava gave her an annoyed glance. "You know damned well it was us."

Giovianni, stationed beside the door, looked around the living room and said in a voice of discovery, "Hey, when I took the census they told me three nuns lived here but I see only two."

Grassia snapped his fingers. "There's your answer, Frank, your men missed a room and there's some nun playing hide-and-seek with us."

"So find her," Scozzafava said, glaring at Giovianni. "She'll have to be upstairs or we'd have seen her steal the sugar off the stairs. Christ it's hard to get reliable help these days."

Grassia nodded. "They don't know the meaning of work any more, all they want is the money. Not like the old days, is it Frank?"

"You can say that again," Scozzafava told him gloomily. "The Puritan ethic's shot to hell."

From upstairs came a triumphant shout and the group in the living room exchanged anxious glances. Sister John said quietly, "You don't think—"

"He could have," said Brill. "Who else would they have found?"

"The damn fool—he's just greedy enough," put in Alfie.

Shouts of laughter floated down from the upper staircase. Giovianni shouted, "Boss, you'll never believe who we found dressed like a nun and hiding all the snow in a closet. You won't believe it."

"Try me and see," Grassia told him sharply. "Stop the games and come downstairs."

Three people slowly made their appearance on the stairs, their shoes first—one pair looking very familiar—followed by two pairs of pants on either side of a long and flowing skirt. They reached the bottom of the staircase and presented to the world a disheveled and panic-stricken Sister Ursula.

"Everett Brown!" gasped Grassia.

"In the flesh," said Giovianni, grinning.

"*Who?*" asked Sister John, walking into the hall to join them. "Who did you say this man is?"

"My accountant. *Was* my accountant," Grassia said, and walking over to Sister Ursula hit him hard across the face with the back of his hand. "Stool pigeon," he growled. "What d'ye mean, who is he, you been hiding him, haven't you?"

"We found him bleeding to death in a closet," she told him coldly, "and I'll have to ask you not to hit any guest of ours in this house."

"Hey, I know that name," Alfie said, joining her in the hall. "He's the guy who was in all the papers last week; I remember the headlines. The Mafia accountant who turned state's witness, right? He was on his way to the court house from jail—under heavy guard, too—and he was kidnaped right from under the noses of the marshals."

"Bright boy," said Grassia, and turning to Scozzafava said, "Frank, you mind doing me a favor and lending me your hit man?"

"Not at all," Scozzafava said, and with a nod to Charlie, "Kill the man, Charlie. Finish him off."

"I won't allow you to shoot Sister Ursula again," said Sister John, looking pale but resolute. "Sister Hyacinthe went to a great deal of trouble to save his life, and it's out of the question that you shoot him again."

"Out of whose question?" said Scozzafava rudely. "Get it over with, Charlie, we've got a busy night ahead. Start with Ev Brown but for Christ's sake use a silencer, I'm very sensitive to noise."

"Has it occurred to you that Sister Ursula—I mean Mr. Brown—may be sensitive to getting killed?" demanded Sister John. "Gentlemen, think of the Golden Rule, think of your consciences, it must already be the Sabbath Day by now."

"You think of it, Sister," said Scozzafava in a dangerous voice. "Go ahead, Charlie, show what a real hit man can do."

Charlie brought out his gun and fitted a silencer to it with expert fingers. He stood with his back to the front door, a distance of six feet between him and a cowering Sister Ursula.

"Charlie is not going to shoot anyone," said Sister John quietly, and began to walk slowly across the hall toward him holding out her hand. "Give me the gun, Charlie."

Charlie grinned. "Better stay back, Sister, I've shot twenty-three people already." He lifted his gun and aimed it at Sister Ursula, clinging desperately to the newel post.

Sister John continued walking toward him, her face calm, her voice gentle. "Give me the gun, Charlie."

Alfie said, "For God's sake somebody stop her, she's moving into his line of fire."

"We mustn't," whispered Sister Hyacinthe behind him. "She wouldn't like that, you know, she has perfect faith."

"The gun, Charlie," repeated Sister John, advancing on him, her eyes fixed upon his.

"For Chrissake get her out of my way," shouted Charlie. "Boss, how can I shoot Ev with a nun in the way?"

"Then shoot her too," said Scozzafava furiously. "Go ahead, shoot."

"Ave Maria, gratia plena; Dominus tecum: benedicta tu in mulieribus, et benedictus fractus ventrie tui Iesus," murmured Sister John, and came to a stop in front of Charlie, still holding out her hand. She said, "The gun, Charlie."

He stared at her as if hypnotized.

"Shoot, Charlie," screamed Scozzafava. "For Chrissake shoot. Look, has anybody else a gun? Somebody give me a gun and I'll shoot the lot of them. Charlie, for the last time—*kill!*"

Charlie and Sister John faced each other for an endless, pregnant, spellbound moment. No one moved or breathed. At last the silence was broken almost ludicrously by the sound of glass shattering in the living room. A man jumped through a window, followed by another. The front door flew open, knocking Charlie to his knees, and from outside a voice called over a loudspeaker: "This is the FBI speaking, we have the house surrounded. . . . This is the FBI speaking, we have the house surrounded. . . ."

The second man to plunge through the front door was Quigley carrying a machine gun. "Okay," he shouted, "hands over your heads, everybody—Weathermen move to the left and Black Liberation Army to the right. . . ."

Epilogue

"Well, I think that's about it," said Sister John, studying the kitchen with a critical eye. She noticed a dried mustard blossom under the sink. "Do you have the list there, Sister Hyacinthe?"

Pencil in hand Sister Hyacinthe began reading it aloud, ticking off the entries one by one. "Five sheets of inventory. House keys. Safe-deposit keys and receipt. Soup kettle. Books. Herbs. Including," she said with a glance at the bare ceiling, "twelve bags of drying mustard."

"And garbage," added Sister John, removing the bag from under the sink. "Unless," she said with a glance at Alfie, "you'd like the eggshells?"

"You can keep them," Alfie told her generously. "I must say we're going to miss Quigley, though. Last night we had to drive all the way to the town dump with our bottles and cans."

Sister John shook her head. "I still find it incredible that you've been under surveillance for a year because of that book. It's the most preposterous thing I've heard of."

"Brill's a dangerous man," said Naomi with a grin.

"But for more than a *year*?"

"Well, you know how they explained it," Naomi reminded her. "Quigley's reports got buried in the files, the computer automatically kept sending pay checks to him and even after Quigley decided Brill wasn't going to blow up the Pentagon nobody read his reports or thought to call him off. It must have hurt Quigley's feelings terribly to discover he was a forgotten man."

"It's an insane world," said Sister John.

"Yes, and welcome back to it," Brill told her with a grin.

"But really I don't think Quigley came out of this badly," protested Alfie. "Once he recovered from the initial shock, of course. After all, with Sister Ursula back in the witness stand today testifying about IRS statements they'll soon have Grassia on tax evasion charges. . . . They caught Scozzafava ordering Charlie to commit murder, not to mention unable to explain fifty pounds of cocaine on the premises. Of course I don't know who they'll arrest for the nineteen bodies buried in the back yard . . ."

"And to think I planted herbs over two of them," said Sister Hyacinthe.

"Nice touch, though," pointed out Naomi.

"But I'm going to go on worrying about Sister Ursula," admitted Sister Hyacinthe. "We worked so hard over him and people keep wanting to shoot him. It's no wonder he couldn't trust anyone and asked for sanctuary. What will happen to him?"

"Actually the FBI explained that to me last night," said Sister John, "and I've not had a moment to tell you. They're going to give him a new identity and new credit cards—apparently credit cards are very important—and set him up as an accountant in another part of the country. One can only wish they could provide him with a new character, too," she added with a sigh. "I've advised him to marry. He's only forty-one, you know, and there's still time."

"Always in there pitching," said Alfie admiringly.

"Of course." Tucking her bedroll under her arm she walked into the main hall and stopped, looking around her. The house was silent, the sun streaming through polished windows, bees murmuring outside in the wisteria. "This is a *good* house now," she said with feeling, "and later we'll make it even better. Where's Bhanjan Singh?"

"Outside with Melida and Alice."

She nodded, and gesturing them ahead of her closed the door behind them, turned the key in the lock and firmly shut the screen door.

Melida was waiting anxiously on the bottom step with Alice at her side. "You won't forget us, ma'am?"

"Of course I won't," Sister John told her in a shocked voice. "I've addressed and stamped a dozen envelopes for you, Melida. . . . Here they are, see? I want to hear from you every month so that I'll always know where you are and I can write you how matters are progressing. It'll take time, you know, two years at least."

Melida shook her head. "It don't matter, ma'am, so long as there's something to keep us glued together. We'll even come and sleep in tents if you say so."

"Tents," murmured Sister John, looking thoughtful. "What a clever idea! Brill, had we discussed tents at all?"

Over by the van Sister Hyacinthe was pressing a bouquet of herbs into Bhanjan Singh's hand. "There's rose-mary for remembrance, and comfrey for healing, and yarrow for divination, and after meeting you I shall never feel lonely again."

He smiled and helped her to climb up behind the wheel of the van. " 'A lamp has no rays at all in the face of the sun,' " he said, " 'and a high minaret even in the foothills of a mountain looks low.' Will you be happy to return to St. Tabitha's?"

She nodded. "The elderberries will be in bloom, you know, and I won't have to wear shoes all the time."

Sister John, standing bemused in the center of the driveway said, "We really must go but it's *such* a wrench. Still," she added, brightening, "we'll have so much to tell them at St. Tabitha's, won't we, Sister Hyacinthe?" Comforted by this thought, she tossed her bedroll into the van and climbed in beside it. Looking radiant, she leaned forward and called, "It's been such a glorious experience, hasn't it?"

The engine abruptly roared into life and the van lurched forward, narrowly missing Alfie. Sister Hyacinthe stopped smiling and grabbed the wheel with both hands. "Good-by—God bless you," shouted Sister John, and slowly the van moved down the driveway to enter the trees lining Fallen Stump Road.

" 'A glorious experience,' " echoed Alfie dryly. "I'm still wondering what could have happened—what *did* happen—between Sister John and Charlie. Especially after it turns out that he cold-bloodedly murdered thirty-six people instead of twenty-three. Can anyone explain it?"

"I think," said Naomi solemnly, "that it had to be perfect faith—you heard Sister Hyacinthe. And I don't," she added fiercely, "see what else it could have been, do you?"

The sound of the van faded in the distance and they stood silent, reflecting, until Alfie straightened his shoulders and said, "Well, no sense in just standing here, it's time to get to work on tomorrow."

"Yes," said Bhanjan Singh, and turning for a last glance at the trees behind which the van had disappeared, he said softly, " 'For we are waves whose stillness is non-being. We are alive because of this, that we have no rest.' "

Discover—or rediscover—Dorothy Gilman's feisty grandmother and fearless CIA agent . . . Mrs. Pollifax!

~

~

Published by Fawcett Books.
Available wherever books are sold.